The Jealous Ear

THE
Jealous Ear
A NOVEL BY
Robert Early

19 BOSTON 73
Houghton Mifflin Company

First Printing   w

ISBN: 0–395–17115–6
Library of Congress Catalog Card Number: 72–12398
Printed in the
United States of America

for

George Herndl
Philip O'Connor
Anne Lyons
and for
Old Jake

Surely men of low degree are vanity, and men of high degree are a lie: to be laid in the balance, they are altogether lighter than vanity.

PSALM 62

. . . and the madness of touch on a blighted world will be the heal of it.

FREDERICK ECKMAN

The author gratefully acknowledges the influence and assistance of William Brammer, Elizabeth McKee, and Dorothy de Santillana.

The Jealous Ear

* 1 *

IT WAS A CERTAIN SUNDAY in 1938. We DeWhits, being
the first family of the town of Kornelius-Above-the-
South-Shoals, had got ourselves off to Jerusalem the
Golden Memorial Church where it was our custom to be
an example to the Christian Service. Since Grandfather,
Robert S. DeWhit, operator of the famous DeWhit Industries, owned the town and owned the church, he did
not really need to keep up with anybody, but he was
there just the same. He was regarded as a prophet as
well, and given the place of honor in the red-cushioned
pew up front. My sister Elizabeth and I were with him,
but Mother and Grandmother DeWhit were not; they
sang in the choir where you had a better view of what
was going on.

As I was awakening to the meaning of words and to
certain other manifestations of my own sensibilities, I

had got to thinking that the Christian Service was not very practical. For example, I could not understand how Great-aunt Beans Duncan, the most practiced of the believers there (next to Grandmother DeWhit herself), could get up the way she often did and shout two *hallelujahs* without knowing what the word meant. Besides, if it were true, as the Reverend said, that going to heaven was a slow and painful process (enough to take you a lifetime), why not say only one *hallelujah* one Sunday and another the next?

I watched my grandmother's large coarse sister, nonetheless, wondering if her words might have a secret message, and she bobbed back and forth and continued her responses (if not *hallelujah,* then *praised be;* if not *praised be,* then *Jesus saves*) like a strutting goose; and the eyes, dark and lively, moved in a strange but visible delight.

Before us, the Reverend Austin Brendelle preached a sermon called "The Passage of Light and Its Latter Day Wonder." But he first provoked the wails of the congregation's women as though he had got them in a secret contest for the best of the penitential tones. Once he had done that he attacked the air which flew out of responding throats before him as if he were fanning off the sour-smelling stink of a punctured inner tube. This dark Reverend, given to quarrels with my grandfather's sins and to crusades against the drug called Pepsi-Cola (especially against my sister Elizabeth's alleged association with Nigger Ruth the Prophetess's girls who were

known to consume that drug and were nothing but
Presbyterian whores), said on this particular Sunday
that the salvation of the Lord lay in the awakening of
the spirit. He did not say when or where, not even how
or why, but Great-aunt Beans was willing to back him
up. She swelled her great mill hand's bosom like an ex-
plosion. Then chose, "Praised be!"

"And that is hardly the full picture either," the Reverend went on.

"Praised be!"

"Nor is it ever to be!"

"Praised be!"

"And the truth will out!"

"Hallelujah and Praised be!"

You were aware mostly of the great puffs of breath
which it took to get all of that out. You heard the
sound of the broken organ blower whir against the hu-
midity. Last of all, there were all the curious movements
which the buttocks of churchgoers make when they
slide with the tedium of being collectively bored.

Everything was meeting with the Reverend's approval, however, the presentiment being his regular
glances toward the tallest diapason tubes of the back-
gallery pipe organ which seemed to give him additional
inspiration and which were actually fake. He virtually
always needed to be guided by the spirit, or at least he
said, "I need to be *guided*." He said it with the customary flair, with assurance, though the Reverend also
spent careful moments, between lines, looking not to

offend his employer. And Grandfather sat there as if he heard everything. His mouth was pooched out in a special prophetical pout, and his ashen face glowed omnisciently.

What we all knew was that the old patriarch actually slept, and watching him, and having in mind first of all to discover what it might come to if the Reverend ever did call on him to explain himself, I also thought that Grandfather must be dreaming things which were far-away, as prophets must, and things which ought to have been said but could not be.

What did I really know of him?

He owned the town all right, because Grandmother DeWhit had told me so. He had this strange power over the Reverend Brendelle which I had figured out for myself. Some said that my grandfather was more than a prophet even, but most, if you asked them, would simply tell you, yes, that he *owned* the town. They, like my grandmother DeWhit, said that I would grow up to take his place too, and they said, once in a while, that soon I would own his Memorial Church. They said Robert DeWhit's grandson would come to that church and they said that one day perhaps his grandson's father, Egan Fletcher, would come there too.

Then I was thinking entirely of my father, who was not there, and whom I had never consciously seen. Whose name, like Grandfather's prophecy, had lately got to being another question to my sensibilities. I watched Grandfather attentively, listening, hoping that his faint snore would not get so loud as to bother the Christian Service, and then there was only just this next question: who is my father? Who is Egan Fletcher?

All I really knew of him was what you could gather from overhearing conversations between my mother and Grandmother DeWhit. The latter whispered often that he was "g-o-d-d-a-m-n-e-d" — she spelled (I knew it was a bad word for this reason) — then proceeded to say, hush-hush, "You know, Emma, how evil Egan Fletcher is, how he came here and messed you up under the pine tree. Do you want *that* again?" As we lived with Grandmother and Grandfather DeWhit, we were beholden and obliged to agree with their prescriptions, and so Mother probably said, "Oh well." She would have embraced Grandmother, too.

I was thinking that there were other little things as well. I had, for example, discovered Father's letters to Mother. I knew they were his because I could read my own name in those days. And she kept them hidden in a secret scrapbook under the twelfth table napkin in the foyer linen closet of my grandfather's house. When she found me with them, she snatched them away quickly and said, "There's vengeance deserved for those who pilfer. You are not to do that again."

I said, "I do not know what that word means. I do not know what any of this means, and where is he?"

She had hit me then and wandered off in her gentle way, wearing a chiffon housedress of gold and crying secretly.

I did not wonder about it without remembering how Mother had looked that time. She had drawn her face up to mew like a cat, and there was a look of futility as if she were trying to catch the movement in the second hand of a clock. She always had that look, especially when she was supposed to be tender or when, for any reason, she was called upon to console or comfort. And in those days she was the one who most often had to comfort Grandmother DeWhit who had her problems with old Grandfather as well. Prophetical though he was, he was given to saying words which Grandmother DeWhit could only spell because they were evil; and sometimes he urinated in the foyer waste-can when he would come home from his cotton mill too heavy to make it to the toilet. On those occasions Grandmother would cry out, "Oh dear"; she would say that Psalm which goes, "I will endure," and so forth, then run to my mother for comfort. It was then that Mother would look that way which made me think of Father.

Other mysteries as to his whereabouts had to do with my sister Elizabeth's remark that he was "paradoxically inclined." Elizabeth was fourteen then and she was sophisticated beyond imagination, often able to quote from her favorite ladies' magazines from memory. Besides that, she wore jodhpurs, knew many speeches from Shakespeare, and rode her hobbyhorse named Integer Vita. She would not, however, tell me anything about Daddy Egan (he was called that to distinguish him from Grandfather, Daddy Robert) except that he was richer and more famous than Grandfather. She said, "And besides, you are too young and so silly that you wouldn't understand anyhow."

Once every so often, my father's three sisters, who were apparently fond of him, would come from his own town of Vermen close by, on pilgrimages inquiring as to his whereabouts (even though they knew he was not there with us), only to be chased away by Grandmother DeWhit because they did not dress to suit her, she said. And because they were what she spelled, "w-h-o-r-e-s."

But for the indirect remarks from Grandmother (as when she would say that the Fletchers of Vermen did not wash their fronts and were dealers in spells) that was all you knew. And that was all that I thought.

It was all that I could bring to mind there in church, though the Reverend's sermon was not yet finished and Grandfather DeWhit had waked up and was no longer a threat to the peace. I smiled at the old man, but he did not return the smile; he did not notice me; and then I saw that my mother was looking at him specially from ahead in the choir cage. She was looking in that same way she looked when I had found the scrapbook with Father's letters. The futile little stare was ever so complete this time, as you noticed that she was as well steadying Grandmother DeWhit, who sat next to her in the alto section of the choir and looked infuriated.

What you saw then was that old Grandfather, according to another of his customs, was shamelessly making sweet and imploring faces toward Great-aunt Beans Duncan. He almost blew her kisses, in fact, and while you knew that the patriarch undoubtedly did what he did as the owner of many things, you suddenly knew as well that he was doing it at Grandmother DeWhit's expense. She was aware of what was going on between the old man and her sister, and soon enough she was also crying about it.

As for the problem itself, I was thinking that you could not be sure in those days since Grandmother De-Whit and Aunt Beans had always had a peculiar association. And what I mean is that Grandfather DeWhit, fond of rhymes in his special way, called the former "Zip" and the latter "Zap." And he said, "One good in the grip and the other in the lap."

Whatever it meant, you often found the two women together in the kitchen of Grandfather's house sipping coffee politely, and they would eventually break off at a certain time when Beans would say, "Oh these are sad times, dearie; this is not time for the fun which we used to have, and there is this dread European war coming on." Then Aunt Beans would go home to the Mill Hill, down behind Grandfather's house, where she sat on her front porch swing and raised her hands so that you could see how fat she was and how black were her underarm hairs. As it was summertime, she called her lame son Clyde, who came off the Vermen road from selling coat hangers about that time of day and gave his mother a secret Pepsi-Cola.

For her own reasons, Grandmother DeWhit would have been watching from the kitchen window, and as soon as Clyde gave obese Aunt Beans her drink and turned around and started to pick at his enormous groin (which was famous for its time), Grandmother would say, "Look at that! How disgusting!" Then she spelled, "B-i-t-c-h, Beans is just a b-i-t-c-h."

The apparent conflict over hygiene and over Grandfather's affection was what I had figured out in my sensibilities. But presently it was more heightened than ever and Grandmother DeWhit started to yell her part of the choir tune (the very famous piece of Haydn's called "The Basic Firmament") and she used the attention she got to bring a glare on Great-aunt Beans.

Then it was time for Mother to give Grandmother DeWhit some special comfort. She looked at the older woman with that little futile stare that I have mentioned. What happened was that Mother also said those words which were generally the last resort, those words which go: "Noblesse oblige, Mama," and for all the odd wonder of it, Grandmother was quiet. She would always fidget a little and her face would get red like a ringworm scale, but then she would smile a little and, if Grandfather happened to be looking, she gave him a nod.

Which she did this time for certain because everyone was aware of her anger and everyone knew that it was time for old Grandfather, in his capacity as patriarch, to rise for his customary Sunday testimonial. In the

church the air was quite as soft as the day, which was
outside pushing forth like summer out a water trough;
but the prophet's imposing voice boomed out very nearly
over the whole town of Kornelius (everybody was there
anyhow except maybe Nigger Ruth and her girls). He
said, "Well you all know that I own this town and if it
wasn't for me none of you would have jobs. I don't
take credit for this, as it is God himself who sent me. I
am the servant of the Infinite Ply. I am plying God's
trade, ha, ah ha.

> I am the servant of the Infinite Ply
> and I will do his will till I die,

Ha, ha, ha, ha!"

As Grandmother DeWhit was accustomed only to
doing the right thing over Grandfather's rhymes, and so
were all we DeWhits, she would have forbidden us to
laugh with him even though he might have himself
wished us to. And so the curious eye exchange which
went on between my grandparents at that point was but
another of the matters that played on my sensibilities.

The prophet took his great delight in both the rhyme
and in his authority, however. He also delighted in
throwing a few more winks out toward Great-aunt
Beans who only looked at Grandmother DeWhit with a
certain power. And that had signaled the end of the
Christian Service for then. We would have got ready
to get in Grandfather's gray Hudson automobile and
ride imposingly the 200 yards or so that it took us to get

from the Church Hill, across the river which was between the church and Grandfather's house, up to Grandfather's hill itself.

From the Memorial Church we exited with handshakes and with post-Service gentility, whined upon by the Reverend Brendelle, whose favorite parting mew was "Wie geht's." I must say that the old patriarch incautiously told him that he ought to find better words to be smart with, seeing as how the Germans were out to make pismires of the American Republic. "The Infinite Ply is definitely on our side!" he said. He laughed and laughed, but the Reverend did not, though the expression seemed a conscious effort to avoid overtones which might betray what he really thought. Watching Mother and Grandmother DeWhit come from the choir dressing room, their eyes awash with the silver residue of tears, he dipped his response out in satisfied spurts, like foamy suds out a syringe.

He said, "But you must remember, Brother DeWhit, that we are all brothers in Christ, though there is nothing of it in the government and no mention of it 'mongst the military."

Then old Grandfather did what he has always done best and he put up his lonely eyebrows, like a pitchfork in the air, and said, "Hogwash, Austin, son."

He cast a final derisive eye toward the Reverend and toward his ancient wife, who shuddered.

"Hogwash and shit!"

Then we DeWhits went on.

※ **2** ※

IN MY GRANDFATHER'S HOUSE Grandmother DeWhit wound all the clocks. It was her regular and quickest insulation against the behavior of the old prophet that she kept all fifteen of her special timepieces synchronized, polished, and striking. Next to her concern for public morality, which was manifest when she said, "Too few are behaving in church as they ought anymore, and I have made an agreement with the Reverend Brendelle to confess long hours of concern about it," she claimed the care of the clocks as her most important household undertaking. From the prophet Daniel, too, she took her motto: *Time and times and the dividing of times.*

She clucked it as though getting the words out ought to have saved her the trouble of any more anger.

As soon as we had got home from church, she took from me the brass key with a handle cast in rosettes and merlins, which belonged to the mantel clock in the parlor, and affixed it to the face of the largest of her treasures. Her hand turned in precise governed movements, and, somehow, both she and the clock had got recharged.

Holding the cedar box which contained the assortment of keys, in order, numbered and tagged, I followed along behind her and gave her the key that she desired.

"Sweet clock," she said, as though now it were her only companion.

Grandmother's regular attention to the clocks was otherwise less expedient. It was a task that she attended to at set hours on unvarying days. The stations and the times, except those which were provoked on account of Grandfather, were also unvarying, and even before I knew for sure that I could read, I was aware of the literal contents of the table which proclaimed, in Grandmother's handwriting, misspellings and all, THE SKHEDULE OF CLOCKS OF MRS ELLA MAE DEWHIT WIFE OF ROBERT S DEWHIT:

time piece	location	skhedule	our
the Nipoleon	dining room	once the week	9 A.M.
the 3 face clocks	bedrooms upstairs	every day dailey	9:30 A.M.
the great Lewis XIV	parlor	once the week on Thurz	12 noone

the 2 musicale clocks	Mrs Emma De Whit Fletchers room Mrs Ella Mae DeWhits room	same as above	1 P.M.
5 guest clocks	the five guest rooms	every other day	likewise
kitchen clock	kitchen	dailey	10 A.M.
back porch clock	back porch	dailey	anytime
the Ingram wall clock	Mr Robert S DeWhits parlor room		Mr DeWhit will see to the winding himself

The last entry, however, regularly had the effect of getting her upset. And she cried over it. Often she stood before the door of his back parlor (where no one but he ever entered, and which he kept locked even when he was in it) and listened, then tried the handle twice. Since she could not ever manage to get the door opened, she stared at the floor. She went away crying, "Close the lid, give me the box, child, lest my frame of mind be destroyed." Having taken the keys from me, she mumbled loudly enough to be heard, but I could never tell what else it was that she said.

❀

For all the time that Elizabeth and Mother and I had lived in Grandfather's house, I had not yet found out what really went on between my grandparents. Old Grandfather would only be there appreciably on Sundays, and then you knew he was down in that back parlor. You heard him practicing his church testimonies and of course you knew that he had long talks with Great-uncle Fred Duncan, Aunt Beans's husband and the overseer at the cotton mill; sometimes he would, of a Saturday, give a speech for the Chamber of Commerce.

But as for really *seeing* him and *hearing* him, you had to wait for those times when he presided over supper aloft his damask chair at the head of the table (then he would only say "The Infinite Ply has done this meal and we must be thankful, amen"), or else catch him at church where such things as I have already described went on.

But for those clashes, Grandmother DeWhit was the one who ruled the house in his absence, and she said, "I am the queen of the household, and you must not forget child, that you are a DeWhit." Straightening her upswept hairdo, she cried as well: "Oh Daddy Robert, Daddy Robert, when will you ever . . ."

As Grandmother apparently did care for Grandfather in her own way, she also amassed a curious measure of display to prove it. We lived in his twenty-five-room house alongside vases and pedestals and bronze statues, urns, gilded picture frames, which seemed altogether unnecessary when it was hard to find a place to sit, and when most of what could be sat upon could also not be touched. Yet she said, "This is the fitting way for the first family of Kornelius to live. It is the only way properly for us to show our gratitude to dear Daddy Robert for what he has done. He has become the owner of a town from scratch. We are the ones of whom art has been made (and so forth), and these treasures are the evidence."

Formally you could say that the pieces *were* high art, among them a French Gothic armory in which Grandmother kept the first fabrics to come out of Grandfather's mill.

"These are the Sacred Bolts," she said, and she had gone and held them up to the light.

There were chairs from the Italian Renaissance as well, and very many footrests. Often a piece would have an attached gold plaque: *If you are interested in this piece go ask about it from Mrs. Robert DeWhit who owns it in her lovely house in Kornelius.* The tags meant that she had lent the business out to the museum in Vermen.

Grandmother pored over her treasures, then, with Mother's help, and she loved them.

But the further consequence was that the DeWhit women also had invented a code by which all of the pieces ought to be appreciated and by which we DeWhits ought to take our election seriously. For as long as I could remember, too, Mother had said that the effect of being the first family was to make "Elizabeth a lady,

you a poet," and she said, "now you think on that,
both of you, and here, Elizabeth, is a pair of yellow
jodhpurs and a fashion magazine." The exact connection between that and the DeWhit possessions was not
ever apparent in those days, but the acts by which we
learned to cope with our election were.

The women had to have models, they said, and for
this they named the Bible and the Christian Service and
Shakespeare their handbooks. They insisted, moreover,
that what you found in such authors and texts as those
was "gentility." Neither of them explained the word, but
the ritual for it had us eating only off formal white china
(which kept Mother and Nigger Ruth busy constantly),
listening to the radio sparsely, and going to the toilet absolutely forbidden the pleasure of grunting. As Elizabeth was to be a lady (by and large she had got to the
point already because she wore the jodhpurs often and
put her hair in a chignon) and I a poet, we had to learn
our lessons from the *Ladies' Home Journal* and Shakespeare respectively; and collectively we were read to
from the Collier's *Abridged Cervantes* as though the
good life *were* what prevailed in Grandfather's house.

Ultimately, however, the code took its sharpest out-
lines from that book called *The Upper Gate,* which fast
suggested that God rewarded the virtues of good
Christian people with money. Then, for Grandfather's
wealth and patronage, the women could only be thankful in the extreme, building out of that gratitude a sys-
tem of daily Bible readings at which the entire house-

hold and whatever guests we had, or hired hands, or even people passing on the property, were bound to give thanks and hear the consoling prophets. For this we sang hymns and lighted candles and took turns at reading. Elizabeth recited the books of the Bible, and at last Mother played one of her fine piano pieces, like the "Black Hawk Waltz," to show how God had favored her. She said the concluding prayer, too, and asked if anyone had anything to be thankful for.

"We thank thee, Lord, for the silverware," Elizabeth usually said. And then we meditated on the Infinite Ply.

The Sunday clock chore done, Grandmother DeWhit called us for that afternoon's Bible reading. As Sunday *was* the day on which Grandfather spent appreciable time with us, and so the day upon which the routine could be varied for the sake of a little entertainment, we were down there in the great parlor where the air smelled like a cave on account of the antiques, and, first, you heard Grandmother say, "Tonight we shall have a little Bruckner before the service in honor of God's beauty and God's frame of mind, which readily sends forth beauty even out the face of *expunged* public morality." She looked at Grandfather fiercely, and he returned her stare as if his lip had been the gauze falling off an old sore.

"Does it please you, Daddy Robert?" she asked.

And he said, "Hell no."

"It is Bruckner's Fourth," she whined. "Robert, it is

his Fourth and the one of which Emma ordered us from Paris, France."

Grandfather scratched his right leg clear of its psoriasis scales, and blew them to the left of his foot, and after he had told her that he had come there only to see to the children's education, that he, in fact, did not care at all for Bruckner but preferred the Infinite Ply in all things ("God alone knows such stuff as your beauty and your truth, woman"), he had also got up and lighted his pipe and went away to feed the chickens that he kept.

Which made Grandmother DeWhit more distraught than I had ever seen her. She looked defiant, and she said, under her breath, sarcastically, "Him and his old Infinite Ply." She called after him, letting the last of her three-syllabled pronunciation of his name slide gruffly downward, mannishly.

"Daddy Robert, come back here. Daddy Robert, I mean . . . come back here, please!"

Though it was not uncharted terrain, Grandmother DeWhit came perilously close to complaining to him over it. Usually she only went, after such an exchange, to the kitchen where she commenced to slam the re-frigerator door. Ultimately, she found at least one clock that could have been wound a half turn.

This time she was only going self-piteously around the room in her cries, and that was not new except that it was very loud and then she wore the look of anticipation she would have when she worried about one of the clocks needing repair. She knew nothing about hours and moments beyond their connection with springs winding and bells striking. She ultimately cared little for time; the important thing was the necessity of measuring it. Just now the real story on Grandfather was the same: she only wanted the patriarch *there;* she did not seem to care what his presence meant.

Grandmother's eyes at length grew wider, and she sat next to Mother for her usual comfort.

"Oh, children," she whined, "do overlook this feeling in your grandmother of which you should not see."

She put her hand out toward Elizabeth and me. She closed her fingers tightly into a fist and withdrew it over the unplayed recording of Bruckner's *Seventh* Symphony.

"Noblesse oblige," Mother whispered elegantly, her head twisting in gentle motion; Grandmother yielded her tears to mere sniffing.

"His activity is hardly defensible, after all," Grandmother whined. "I have given him this lovely house, and . . ."

Mother said, "Hardly defensible." She said it moving on her footrest, rubbing her chin with the top of her soft yellow housedress. She looked at Elizabeth and me as well, and then she and Grandmother DeWhit went on with their conversation.

"His action is no more defensible than Nigger Ruth the Prophetess's handling of the linens, Emma. There have been spots on the table linens, two soiled counterpanes, frayed tablecloths, three improperly ironed napkins. It does so spoil my frame of mind," Grandmother said.

Mother said, "Noblesse oblige" until Grandmother sighed and repeated it too. She said the Psalm, "I will get me to my mountain," in preparation for the Bible reading. She was embarrassed to look in the direction by which Grandfather had exited.

The women had rubber faces, though, for a time, Mother's was less pliable. It was more than generally certain, moreover, that she had in mind something more than her duty to moderate the ancient battle between the old prophet and his wife. Her look of helplessness is what I really noticed, and I thought that she might have been looking for my father to help her bear up.

* 3 *

Now AUNTS MAGGIE, MYRA, AND WEXIE FLETCHER were
Father's sisters. They came out of the town of Vermen
from time to time, as I have said, to ask where he was
and if my mother was ever to give up what they called
her "widderhood." Mother always said, "I will not discuss this matter with anyone," and they went away without getting any farther than the front door. That was
basically Grandmother DeWhit's doing.

But my aunts were pretty women, I must say. They
looked like Vivian Leigh if you discounted the bumps
on their faces and the Blue Waltz Perfume. They were
chestnut haired and thin; Maggie, the first one, had
peculiar triangular toenails which were painted red and
showed through her open-toed shoes. The women said
things like "tickled pink" and "I swanee." Which one of
them, probably Maggie, said immediately as they stood

that afternoon at the front door with a certain urgency
and with a determination once and for all not to be
turned out. In fact Wexie, who was the brightest and
prettiest of them, put her foot in the door like a vacuum
cleaner salesman.

"We have brung some presents for Mrs. Ella Mae
DeWhit from our mama, Mrs. Willie Bee Fletcher, and
we have brung for you, Emma, the latest scrapbook of
what we have been collecting on Egan," she said.

Loudly chewing gum, they forced themselves past
Grandmother DeWhit, who had only momentarily
finished the last Psalm of the Bible reading, and into
the parlor. Where Wexie went on, "We truly have brung
these presents, Missus DeWhit."

Maggie held out a salve can full of yellow dahlias,
and Myra a Mason jar with white peonies. Grandmother
accepted them into her handkerchiefed hand reluctantly
and put them aside as the sweet-faced women seated
themselves on selected footrests.

They were not speaking. They were oddly preoccupied with pulling at their skirts. Then they quizzi-
cally watched Grandmother DeWhit, aside, pulling at
Mother's dress sleeve and spelling certain words. She
stood by the door jamb out there in the dining room at
last, and she was close to the refrigerator in the kitchen.

What went on was a great many eye exchanges, the
usual silence which you have when people do not
know how to get a conversation started. Finally Aunt
Wexie, biting her bottom lip, held out the black

albumlike book she had brought with her. She looked at Mother like a traffic officer.

"I said we have brung Egan's latest scrapbook and I mean it; here it is, you see," she announced. She turned in my direction and said, "We have brung this one for you, child." She put out a hand, which had Mother suddenly brushing little strings of thread off the lap of her dress.

Expecting to be stopped at any moment, the tight-lipped visitor lifted her arms and read from the front page of her evident treasure:

THESE BOOKS HAS BEEN CAREFULLY COMPANDED IN HONOR OF EGAN FLETCHER OF THE WASHINGTON TEUTONIANS FOR MR FLETCHERS SON EGAN FLETCHER JR BY MISS BONNIE WEXIE FLETCHER SISTER OF THIS MR FLETCHER WHOM IS MENTIONED ABOVE

She looked at me specially well again. She was aware that Mother was grimacing; and her face, powdered to the shade of soda paste, got oddly intense and worshipful. She felt her way up to catch Mother's eyes, touching my face firmly, at the same time, with her long fingers.

"Did you know that your daddy is a player of sports?" she asked. "Did you know that your daddy is a well-known and Christian player of that game called baseball."

"Baseball?" I said.

Aunt Wexie pointed to a small monogrammed triangle painted in the lower left corner of the scrapbook. It was a crest with three pillars. It surrounded a large ball

stitched to a smaller one so that the two balls both inter-
twined and separated. According to Aunt Wexie, it
explained everything, and the inscription read:
FLETCHERS TOGETHER. She said that she had taken an entire day to think of it.

"There's a cartoom of him in one place," Myra said.

And Maggie, chewing her gum like a piece of hot
food, said that she was tickled pink.

All of it caused Mother to pick up the book herself
and she got to paging through it and brushing bits of
dust from it. The color of her face had been suddenly
washed out, too, as she kept looking more and more
helplessly toward Grandmother DeWhit.

The news photos in the album were of a large, heavy-
bodied man whose face you could not see exactly. You
saw the white uniform but it was spotted. Wexie held
a couple of the news photos next to me and said, "Aren't
you interested in your daddy? Aren't *you* even interested in what he is up there in Washington doing for
you? Father and son," she said.

I said, "Washington?" but then I said, "Oh yes, I am
interested."

The burrowing eyes of my aunts, like emergent waves,
drilled me indulgently. They laughed then, though you
could feel the building-up emotions as if they were shifting strategies. You could tell, for instance, that Mother
herself was getting interested in whatever underlay their
little facial gestures. And, for all that, I did not neglect
my own idea either. I was drawn to them as I had been
even on the earlier swifter occasions when Aunt Wexie's

delicate touches had left me feeling strangely con-
tented. When she would come, she always had seemed
to think it her duty to come over to me and put her hand
on my face as if she were getting my temperature, and it
had always been at that point that Mother or Grandmother had got upset and asked them to leave. Of
course they had usually not got past the door anyhow,
and this time they were particularly tense, it seemed,
about avoiding former rituals. Still Aunt Wexie insisted
on this face-touching and I liked it and it caused me to
wish for whatever it was she proposed. In her wistful
smile I had thought to discover Father, perhaps (if that
was what she had wanted), and I made an infusive attachment between her and the photographs where the
large and undefined face was only unmoving. For the
moment I had as well tried to supply the missing smile.

But then Grandmother DeWhit was gritting her teeth
like a dental patient. She came over and forced Wexie
to close the scrapbook. She said, "Get out of here," and
Wexie's eyes fell at what you saw was her own appreci-
ation of the inevitable. She looked at the ceiling; and
Grandmother, with all the neck motion of a circus
barker, had tried to lure Mother's eyes out toward the
pine trees. She had also begun to shake and then she
moaned.

"Oh, Emma, dear, you just must not have those
thoughts and you must not just let these — influence
you this way. I can tell, and . . . remember the pine
tree."

Then the movement of fourteen feet was like splattering bowling pins on the marble foyer floor, and that was where the gathering went in dispersal. It seemed that no one had wanted to face whatever it was they were all aware of. Let alone Mother, who held Grandmother's hands and embraced her and said, "Noblesse oblige, Mama."

Grandmother said, "Oh, I am so glad, dear. You have not weakened, Emma, and they have not done their evil."

Mother said, "I *know* what you are trying to do, Mama." She said it sternly, and held on for as long as Grandmother wanted.

In the following silence the visitors, somehow embarrassed, prepared to leave. Wexie stood apart; sorry, she said, to have caused the disorder.

Mother held her head high plaintively and pulled her hair behind her ears.

"We did our best," they said.

Aunt Wexie went on saying how much a shame it all was, how much, in fact, the children must need a father and how somehow they ought to be free from . . .

The decisive glance cast at Grandmother DeWhit had only infuriated the queen of the household further and Wexie then thumped her own foot on the marble foyer. She was nervous, but at last she went over there to Mother and put her arms around her too.

Before Grandmother DeWhit could displace any of it, Wexie said, making it a speech:

At least the boy needs his father; you see, don't you, Emma, that the boy needs his Daddy Egan.

Mother dusted her dress without putting her arms around Wexie, and she gave Grandmother a look which restrained her. Everybody stood only momentarily as if each were making his own decision, though in Mother's and Grandmother's faces you saw a repulsion as they listened to the noise of the visitors' chewing gum.

All the while there, this man in the photographs had got to be the breath of it, however. And his image, at least to me, was the thing which went on and on. Aunt Wexie held out the scrapbook, which Mother rejected and which she also prevented me, by holding me, from accepting. The few things which I knew about him thereupon passed, in the movement of the book, from one aunt to the other, and finally out the door where Maggie took it as though she had the cornerstone that the builders rejected.

I said, "I want to see him, Mama; please, can't I see him?"

But with Grandmother coming unglued again like that and wincing and scraping her own arm with finality, Mother ignored me and guided the last two Fletcher women out the door.

They, themselves, were unbelieving, you could tell, and they were also speechless but for Wexie's sudden announcement:

Well, whatever, Emma, Egan's coming home to see you. And that's what we really come to tell you.

What you saw was Mother's little smile coming up, but she concealed it quickly from Grandmother DeWhit.

Wexie saw it, and I did, though by then you could hear Grandmother DeWhit out in the kitchen slamming the refrigerator door wildly.

When Father's sisters were gone, she returned to the foyer and held Mother's hand pitifully and mumbled.

Then she said, "What he is really doing, Emma, is coming home to see old Lady Fletcher for his annual titty. Don't be fooled, for, as you know, Emma, dear, he only comes for titty."

With my own thoughts plotted, and with a sense of my own accomplishment, I watched Grandmother De-Whit in utter abandon. She had suddenly noticed me as well, and catching herself in what was apparently one of those words which I was not supposed to hear in those days, she frantically spelled: "I mean t-i-t-t-y, and Willie Bee Fletcher, his mother, is a b-i-t-c-h!"

✳ 4 ✳

THE DAY FOLLOWING, when Aunt Wexie called up on the telephone and told Mother that Daddy Egan was coming from wherever Washington happened to be on such-and-such a day train and that someone would have to meet him at the station in Vermen, Mother mentioned the news first to Grandfather DeWhit, who, standing on the back porch with his leg on the woodshed door as he tied his shoe and got ready to go to the mill, put his hand delicately upon Mother's shoulder and said, "Emma, you get things ready and plan what you want."

At once Grandmother DeWhit, aware by her own devices that a call had come from Vermen, came from the kitchen, moved herself craftily next to Grandfather and fiddled with his shirt collar.

He said, "*You* do what Emma says."

And Grandmother, policelike, her legs clamped together, muttered the Psalm which goes: *Lead me, Oh*

Lord, in thy righteousness because of mine enemies.
She said it in a whisper almost, and drew her collar
tightly around her throat. She clamped her fingers into a
knot, holding them in front of her face; and her eyes,
like the ooze of gelatin, followed Grandfather in his
departure.

She said at last, "*I heard everything.* I am aware of it
and each word of it fairly worries my soul. Why cannot
Egan Fletcher walk from the train station which is
befitting? Why cannot Wexie Fletcher fetch him there?"

Mother said nothing and went to the telephone atop
the chair rail in the hallway where she began calling
in the grocery list. There Grandmother followed with a
crude litany of entreaties, stroking Mother's arm.

"Oh dear, oh dear Lord," Grandmother said. "Don't
be a foolish child," she whined, and Mother went on
with the list. She looked at Grandmother, shushed her.
She called the names of the foods and wrote against
the small rack of grained oakwood beneath the phone
speaker. She wrote resolutely whatever she had to
write.

Finally she stepped back into the kitchen where
Grandmother followed with quiet sobs. The women
sat at either end of the kitchen table. Mother wrote
on and sometimes looked at the ceiling. Grandmother
sometimes put her head down.

I said, "Mother, what is Daddy Egan like? What
must *I* do?" I said it excitedly, and I smiled widely to
show the feeling.

She winked and buzzed a little yawn out from the

edge of her tongue, framing a composure that ignored me and acknowledged me at the same time. She did not appear unhappy to have me call him Daddy Egan.

"First of all," she said, "stand up straight, first of all, and then second of all, you should kiss him."

The manner became slightly indifferent. She kept writing.

"How will I know *when?*"

"Watch, just watch, and the time will come soon enough."

Then Elizabeth entered, sliding her feet against the patterns of the grained kitchen floor. She was singing, as well, and in one of her teasing moods. Elizabeth was often coy, and it was especially her custom to be so when she saw that I was excited about something. Oftentimes she would even prevent me from telling her what I wanted by grabbing me and holding me tightly. On occasion, she would even kiss me wildly and pull me onto the floor where she would tickle me or unbutton my trousers so that she could look at me. Sometimes, she would appear angry in addition to all the other things, but this time, on account of Mother's presence, and Grandmother's, she merely tried to pinch me without their seeing.

When I told her that Father was coming home, she first grew recondite, and then started to laugh.

"Of course it is wonderful," she said. "Perhaps he will take us with him this time, and perhaps he will have something even to say to *you*."

In the past, Elizabeth had always been that way when she talked about him. Besides the times when she simply had refused to speak because she said I was too young, she also had ignored me most of the time.

Wearing her riding habit, she was erect and sober. With the stance which I recognized as the ignoring one, then, she leaned on the edge of the dish cabinet and counted one by one the hairs of her whip, which she carried like a baton.

She was certain she had enraged me.

"Elizabeth," I said, "oh please, Elizabeth, Mother, please tell me *what*. *What* will Father tell me?"

Mother touched me in a nondescript fashion upon the buttocks, being unconcerned for Elizabeth's attitude. She pushed me out of the way, and Elizabeth walked away smiling. She dove off the back porch with a yell, and, with a radiance as well, seated herself at last in the backyard swing. There my sister, waiting for me to come and plead for my answer, rubbed her thumb along the edges of her teeth and slapped her feet against the ground, where the dust rose.

I did not go to her, and I did not say anything to her though I felt vengeful.

When Grandmother DeWhit had left as well, I stayed with Mother and said, "Well, how must I kiss Father, then?"

"It isn't important."

"Will you tell me what to do and when?"

"That isn't important either."

Mother stooped from the sink and pressed down on my shoulders in a pleasant manner. She embraced me so that I could feel the tightness of her breast.

"You will do what you feel like doing," she said. "But first you must truly stand up straight, and you must kiss him."

The sun was on Mother's hair. The glossy black fell into her face in the finest light, and I touched it while the color turned to a soft straw yellow in places. She had about her the look which was my favorite and it was not the usual one which sometimes meant that she was going to hold me for a long time and kiss me as she often did. And it was not the one with which she was accustomed to telling me that I must learn the words for what I was feeling so that I could write them down someday.

"Is Daddy Egan wicked the way Grandmother says he is?" I asked.

"I don't know," Mother replied with faint tears in her eyes. She rose silently and put off the light switch above the sink and she would not talk anymore, and she listened for noises.

With that same look, she had got, that afternoon, into Grandfather's Hudson under the pecan tree, and we were ready to fetch Daddy Egan. But for Elizabeth's sudden remark that he was truly a great man, there was otherwise no festivity in our going.

Grandmother DeWhit, afoot the running board with

a hand wound carefully about the hems of her skirts, said, "I am only going to this silly train station on an errand of mercy akin to the long hours that I spend in concern for sinners." She then boarded as well and tapped her gloved fingers on the seat of the car, next to Grandfather; and she played with a monogrammed handkerchief the color of her suit with gray stripes, while the old man watched silently the coils of her amethyst ostrich plumes tickle the ceiling of his automobile.

He grunted. And Mother watched his dead-set eyes reflected in the rearview mirror for encouragement, it seemed, and held my hand in the back seat. All the while she grew more remote.

Then we were at the train station in Vermen, and the first thing Mother said was, "Now just stand up straight." She quickly fastened all the buttons of her linen coat and blew the weave to the left.

The second thing she said was, "This is an important occasion. Be calm. First stand up straight, and then kiss him."

Grandmother DeWhit said, "Lord knows this is the kind of a place you would expect to find Egan Fletcher. Look at what is scrawled over there on that door, a filthy word!"

Thereupon you sensed the cultivated chill in the station and you heard brief mechanical noises outside where the tracks were. Bunched together, we hurried around carts. Grandmother DeWhit carried her purse upside down, and Mother swallowed again and again. She looked at Elizabeth and then at me while Grandfather smoked his pipe. Elizabeth and I held hands and walked out into a silver vapor which covered the cement walkway like a thin dust and trailed like smoke out toward the opening of the building, through which several sets of tracks disappeared.

Elizabeth kicked the steam in a game with her patent leather shoes.

At last a single train emerged from an end of the building, hardly able to make it to the middle of the platform where it was apparently expected to stop dead.

Mother said, "He's here," her voice constricted, and the old prophet clasped her shoulder and cleared his throat while Grandmother DeWhit braced herself.

I thought of Mother's instructions, suddenly aware that they did not mean that much. For all the curiosities, I mostly felt the odd longing which Aunt Wexie had put into me. There was an instant about it, to be sure, that I thought I should be someone different or that I should know more than I did. Without provocation from anyone, I ran ahead then, and it was like a moment of breaking away from one of Mother's long embraces.

The one passenger came off the train upon one of those stool-like yellow boxes that the conductor puts out as he looks at his silver watch on the long heavy chain.

This single passenger was upon the box which the conductor put out, surrounded by the steam, with his hand clasped tightly about the railing on the side of the train. He descended backward from the Pullman with a canvas brown coat thrown over his shoulder, a single mahogany-colored suitcase in his right hand. He stepped to the ground with his back to us still, and shook hands with the conductor, losing his footing.

And so I remember well that the first time I saw my father's face, it was in the motion of falling.

But the conductor steadied him, and Father laughed.

His large head bent out of his immense shoulders as if it were hooked there on a lever or a spring. He looked out of a brown coarse face with small intense lines about the mouth and forehead. His eyes were very large and they moved with the same reflective brown. He was not really tall, I noticed, but he looked it as in the photographs. His hair, which was very dry, had a gloss, and there was some of it in his ears.

He said, "Emm." And Mother whispered to herself as well, and waved. Then she ran over there to him and I remember that her hands were digging into the back of his coat as she embraced him at first. But they finally grew limp when he kissed her. In the middle of the kiss they tightened again and then went limp. At last when their bodies appeared to be moving upon each other part for part, Mother had broken away, but with a smile, and Father only just touched her forehead gently.

I could smell him in the faint odor of the train station as he bent over to me at last. It was the smell of spring dirt and a new smell. His breath was especially heavy and piercing and I heard it, like a wind, take the air in my ears toward him. My own eyes were wide. I kissed him fiercely and soberly wished to hold on to the dark motion there. The exclusive warmth cheered even my hands which momentarily caught the L-shaped bone at the back of his ear.

Father took my hand down and pressed it. Holding it, he flew Elizabeth into the air and pulled her to himself and kissed her. It was as if she expected it. She looked triumphant. She kissed him fiercely as well.

I kept Father's hand. The force of something that hard and that full of breath next to me had numbed every impulse but that one which drew me closer. And I must have thought myself indelicate by comparison. At length I resented everyone else there, especially Elizabeth, for it seemed that she had some power over him. He looked at her with a sadness as if he had forgotten me, and then I pulled at his hand again.

"See this, Emm," he said. "The boy has already learned to shake hands. Here, son," he continued, "let's shake hands. Grip, grip, show me that you mean it."

Holding Elizabeth yet, he stiffened the fingers that I held and cupped them around my hand. I pumped hard and laughed though I was still resentful of Elizabeth. He put her down and took her under his arm and walked with us toward Grandmother and Grandfather DeWhit whose faces were like the holes and gaps that the wind makes in leaves. Shadows seemed to fall in patterns according to the movement of the air. My grandparents changed from moment to moment.

Behind us at last the train went off and renewed the endless thin billows of vapor which by now had taken the effect of deep fog in the station house. Grandfather took Father into his arms and shook his hand and patted him upon the arse and then upon the face.

"How many years has it been?" he said.

Father shrugged his shoulders and looked at Mother. "Too many."

He finally looked at Grandmother who, by this time, had well noted her own position as the least of his concerns.

"Mrs. DeWhit," Father said.

"Egan, dear."

"You look well."

"Do I?"

"Yes."

"Well, my frame of mind is disturbed of course."

"I'm sorry to hear that."

"What with the war coming on and having that big house to run."

"Yes, what with the war and all."

"Are you going to tell us what you've come for?"

Grandfather seized his ancient wife's arm as if he had been waiting for the moment. He threatened her with his eyes, and Grandmother DeWhit only nodded in embarrassed submission.

Father stopped cold, however; he said, "Shitfire."

He licked his lip and pointed high with a finger gripped around the handle of his bag. The bag rose. "Hush up, Ella Mae."

Nothing much changed the silence which lasted from there home. Once moving, the Hudson fluttered pepperishly along the road in moves which counted the black grease puddles against the patterned concrete. Father tried to hold Mother's hand, I think, and put his arm warmly around Elizabeth. Mother held me. Off the Vermen road we climbed the entranceway up to Grandfather's house, and before the car had actually stopped, Grandmother DeWhit fled, singing that hymn, "I Will Go to the Garden Alone," signaling me to fetch the clock keys.

I did not like my task because it removed me from Father. I listened and looked all about with every reserve of intensity I had, and then I thought that soon enough I would have to tell him just how it was with us DeWhits.

✳ 5 ✳

BUT MY PARENTS hastily secluded themselves in Mother's upstairs bedroom, where all the food which Mother had ordered was placed. There was an extra bed. Grandmother insisted that it be put there, but Mother had not disagreed. They put it there beside the far window so that it was farther from the door than Mother's bed was.

Mother and Father did not come to supper either, and not even Grandmother's incessant knocks at the door had brought a response. She cried that *it* was happening again.

I was put to bed, in Mother's absence, by Grandmother DeWhit. My thoughts were uncommonly complicated, I believed, but they settled to this: I pleaded to know what Daddy Egan's remoteness meant. "Why," I asked, "could he have been like that to me and then have hid himself away with Mother?"

"*It,*" Grandmother mewed, "*it,*" soberly kissing my forehead, her entire face gathered toward her right ear, where she concentrated on hearing the suddenly emergent dispute from down the hall. You heard loud thumping on a table, and you heard Mother's voice squawking like a blue jay's. Without explanation, but with sudden estimable relief, Grandmother had it that, ah, Mother was in control; she said noise meant that *he* was *not* doing *it*. She said little more than that and sang me to sleep.

In the morning when they had still not come out (and Grandmother had prepared breakfast alone and silently), I went looking for my own explanation of things. I went looking for Elizabeth who seemed presently the only one to ask, and I found her at the fish pond which lay at the front of Grandfather's house, down there ten feet from the left front parapet. As my sister, first of all, was there in her jodhpurs, and singing the song "Lover and Friend" from *The Rose of Sharon,* I knew she did not want to be disturbed. She was thinking her usual thoughts about Clyde Duncan, I perceived, who lately had become what she called her *bow* (she said the word as though it concerned a boat), and who, now for all practical purposes, she declared, made her life an endless song. I knew that she had these peculiar feelings about Cousin Clyde because you could often find them under the nandin bush with their hands on each other. I had seen it, for example, and Elizabeth had made me swear not to tell. It was one reason why she most often ignored me, too, and she said she would kill me if I told. She said that she would fix it so that I would never be able to go to the bathroom again without grunting, and she said, "You know where *that* would get you with Grandmother DeWhit."

The line which I interrupted was "Oh how he does move my soul."

I said, "What is *it*, and where is Daddy Egan?" and Elizabeth looked at me with various types of practiced annoyance.

She said, "How silly are you, Egan!" She leaned her head down against her propped-up knees and giggled. She looked into the fish pond and stirred the water with her horse whip. "He hasn't gone *anywhere*. Besides, what would he want to see *you* for?"

"All I wanted to know," I answered her, "was where Father is." But Elizabeth was inclined only to scoff at me in her omniscient way again and say that they were "doing love." She berated Grandmother's term for it, first, but soon enough had said, cryptically, "Father, more than Mother and better than Grandmother, is rich and famous, and he understands those feelings which people have in their bottom parts."

She got off the ledge and went away. She did not even say anything else and went behind the pecan tree to fetch her stick horse, Integer Vita, which she untied, and rode, bobbing and grazing, around the front yard and down toward the Vermen road.

When Mother and Father at last did emerge, near suppertime, all I had was what Elizabeth had told me and what, subsequently, Grandmother DeWhit had repeated in her otherwise annoyed silence. She said it was a case for the sheriff and the law, which she modified only slightly after old Grandfather, at lunch, had told her to hush up. And so when Mother and Father paused on their way down the staircase to embrace, I did not know what it meant. Moreover, I did not understand at all when, thereupon, Grandmother De-Whit stationed herself beside the refrigerator door, or when Elizabeth, continuing her earlier triumph, came up from the front yard saying:

> I wandered lonely as a cloud
> thou are more lovely and more temperate
> and the darling buds of May
> Ah life!

The truth was that Mother and Father seemed more remote. I placed my hands in front of me and watched them. She was buried in his heavy trunk there on the stairs, and it was a union which for the moment made Daddy Egan darker and stronger than she was. He engulfed her like a black mouth fashioned about a delicate pink interior palate. She hummed an extended note on the letter E, and even from where I stood, I could see that her hands were pushing him away.

At supper you had a stranger kind of silence than the one we were used to. Normally old Grandfather presided and kept looking at his watch. This time he kept winking at Father and then looking at his watch, while Father sat across from me and did little more than say pass this or that. He had a nervous fashion, though, of wiping his mouth each time he spoke, but he always looked at Grandmother DeWhit with a smile. She looked to have the colic, and then complained about Nigger Ruth the Prophetess's job with the table napkins.

She said, "There, see it."

Grandfather said, "Hush up, Ella Mae."

And the point is that, for all its supposed importance, the supper was horrid for everyone, and when Mother and Father retired back to the upstairs bedroom, you got the idea that they were doing it as a favor.

I went to the fish pond ledge and ran my fingers up and down on my lips getting a bubbling sound. Then I clicked my fingers upon the stone ledge one by one getting the sound of horses' hoofs running wildly in an open field. I imagined myself the tamer of horses, the way Elizabeth did often on her hobbyhorse, but with certain sureness that I could not conquer the animals as she did. The game proved unfit and so I pedaled my legs against the ledge then and watched the shadow of their movement. I was thinking about the supper. I was thinking first of Grandmother DeWhit and her displeasure. How she was never happy about anything. How even Nigger Ruth was regularly attacked like that; when, other times, as with Great-aunt Beans, Grandmother would entertain her in the kitchen and would say, "Oh Ruth, oh Ruth," politely and then kiss her.

Perhaps it seemed that Grandmother's fickleness was the only thing in the world which I knew of that never changed. Maybe, I thought, it was for the moment, the only thing which existed before anything else on earth. But everything I thought of turned finally to this: somehow things were not the same.

The ground moved in the shadow of my falling legs against an imagined specter of Grandmother's face. The difference, I saw, was Father. For a time, I recalled that once Grandmother had said, "He is just not here, you see; this is your home, however, and your mother and I are enough."

I did not believe her, and the cords of flesh which propelled my legs in their movement beneath the pond ledge spoke against her. I remembered Father's breath which I had felt at the train station. It was not Mother's tiny breath, or Grandmother's harsh and often sour one. It was not either Elizabeth's hungry breath, but my own firm and constant breath. It was the draft of a law which bound me to Father.

Daddy Egan came out on the porch and called to me.

He said, "Boy, boy, my boy," and he undid his belt and stuffed his shirttail into his trousers while he looked out into the front yard and belched. I scratched my knee, flew myself fast through the great yard, undoing my belt, stuffing my shirt into the top of my drawers. I straightened my socks and looked at him eagerly.

"Are you playing now?"

"No, sir, I was out by the fish pond thinking for myself."

"Come up here."

I climbed the steps quickly and stood in front of him. He looked at me and rubbed the palms of his hands about his chin, and you heard the grind of his whiskers.

He asked me where Elizabeth was, and I told him that she was most likely out riding. I looked for her then, out toward the far end of the yard.

"Riding?" Father questioned. And then, at the same moment, we saw her galloping on Integer Vita.

"A *stick* horse," Father said. He turned his face upward and frowned uncomfortably. Rubbing his whiskers again, he finally lowered his hand to me and I took it to pump. The grip tightened about my hand amicably.

I said, "Elizabeth is a good rider. She also sings and knows many things about the way things are. She is in high school and she plays the clarinet. Elizabeth can say several speeches from the play called 'Othello the Colored Man,' and she knows a declamation, 'The Flag,' by Major W. D. Browne. Soon I will go to school. I already know some speeches as well and I will be in Miss Carlyle's grade, but Elizabeth is in Miss Rosalie's."

Father pressed down on my shoulders. He continued watching Elizabeth and shook his head in a resigned motion. His face softened briefly, though for the moment there was also a frown as his eyes fell again on me. He withdrew his hands soberly.

Then I tried to pull him forward, drawing at his waist like a cat on lace curtains.

"No," he said, waving his hand in restraint. He pulled back momentarily and stared at me. Vaguely smiling, he stretched out a finger to my ear and poked it in. Though he then shook my hand as I wished, he would not allow me to kiss him. Instead, he waved a fist far past the ledge of the porch in a gesture of triumph, up toward the loftiest parapet of Grandfather's house, which was like a black cap clamped to the head of a square-faced old white man, whose eyes looked back and laughed. Father went away into the front yard where he kept walking even after the rest of them had gone to bed.

✻ 6 ✻

As for those words like *it* and *doing love,* there was just one way that I looked at them for the moment: Mother and Father were up there doing *something* in that bedroom. Once Father had left the front yard, you heard the Victrola playing, but most of it was Mother's high, wordless whine.

When I woke up the next morning I found her standing over me saying, "Now get ready because your father wants to take you to Vermen to see your relations."

Father, standing beside Mother but frowning, said, "Ha, ha, son, I just want you to go along with me for a ride." He looked content, but that was all he said.

I said, "What relations will we see in Vermen?" while Mother, then frowning too, looked at him and made a soft sigh like swishing gas. She shifted her eyes back and forth as if to show her indecision on the matter.

"Egan," she said to Father, ignoring my question, "Egan, whatever might the child learn over in that place?" Her hands went nearly wild with further indecision until she had shaken her head. "No," she insisted. "No, I have changed my mind."

She helped to undress me as Father stood and grunted by the chest of drawers. He fingered the three pennies there on the top, and grunted again.

As was Mother's custom, she, quite deliberately ignoring the other presence (but looking at him of course with considerable attention), had me naked and was checking it for impetigo. "You see that he is endowed with much of what you are, Egan, dear," she tried to say indifferently.

But with little less than absolute authority, Daddy Egan seized Mother's arm and kneaded her down to the side of the bed where he told her pointblank that he had decided she was being a goddamned bitch. Which tended to make her wince, though soon enough she had said, "Well take him then. Take him away from his home and his dear mother if that is the kind of a man you are."

I said, "Mother, Mother, what is a goddamn bitch?" And she went to sobbing like a paid mourner until the tremor of it made Father perplexed. The odd burden apparently fashioned odd loyalties too, as they went abruptly about in different directions without speaking.

At length, Father stooped beside me and said, "O.K.,

son, do *you* want to go for a ride?" He put his hand
to my head and thumped the side of it. He smiled
widely, though all the bones in his face seemed only to
soften. I looked at Mother who was pursing her lips
and whimpering, "Do you see what you've done — do
you see what you've done already?" She wrung her
hands anxiously.

"Yes, sir," I said, feeling as if I had been allowed to
grunt on the toilet for the first time.

Then I was dressed and Father had pulled me out
to Grandfather's automobile so breathlessly that I could
feel his pulse against my hand. He first looked sorrowfully into the rearview mirror where you saw Mother
half hiding behind the front screen door of the house.
He told me to wave goodbye to her. He blew his own
kiss toward her, but with the sudden grand motion of
an opened sail.

The first thing he said was "It is true that I have
been in Washington, which is a certain city. I know,
for example, that you do not know about me."

"No, sir," I said.

"Here is what I have to say, then," he continued, his
eyes rising quickly in a soft glide. "I am your father.
I have been away playing the game of baseball, and I
have come back after some time to fetch you and your
sister and mother to be with me. How do you like that?"

"Well, sir," I said, "we have always lived with
Grandmother and Grandfather DeWhit."

What you saw in his face was a little smile accen-

tuated evenly by the funny way that he licked his dry
lips. He did not seem ready to ask anything else for a
time, and the thick moist licking sound became the only
thing that you could hear besides the motor of the
car. It was the sound which I associated with the
butterfly touches that Grandmother DeWhit made with
the soap when she bathed me. She disliked the slimi-
ness she said; especially any sound that went *squeesh*
like soapy water. She had ordered me not to like it
either, and she had also told me once, I remembered,
that *squeesh* was the noise that the Fletchers of Vermen made. "Those sticky Fletchers," she said, "who,
everybody knows, never wash their dirty fronts."

For that Father seemed momentarily an alien brown
in the sunlight. I collected former images of him as if
Grandmother's words had forced me to do so. I thought
of dark photographs in Aunt Wexie's scrapbook while
all along the sound went on; I thought of Mother's dark
and secret letters.

I decided that I had heard the Fletcher sound for
myself. Listening carefully, I thought I had got it
down too. I liked it, and I rolled my tongue awkwardly
about the sides of my mouth to imitate Father.

He moved in his seat, lifting half his buttocks to fart.
He was neither embarrassed nor uncomfortable over
the smell or the sound. Slowly the soupy taint had
crept all over the car. He looked at me knowing that he
had done it.

"God, what an awful smell," he said. And I breathed

soberly with the kind of reserve Grandmother had taught me for such occasions. It was supposed to be the worst, the inexcusable, act to do *that,* she often said. But presently, coming from Father, the inexcusable seemed quite ordinary. When he said, then, "Excuse my fart, son," it was a spirited license too. And I said, "Of course, sir," laughing, laughing and delighted at the viscid energy of it. The former almost visible cord made another unchangeable thing for me to know: I knew that I was an instant older. What happened was that I stretched out my legs and thought myself yawning also. I put my hands between my legs, with my laugh, and pressed the tightness there into bold stretches of growth like elastic.

But for all the satisfaction of the moment I could hear Grandmother DeWhit saying, "How dirty those Fletchers' fronts!" I could hear her praying at the lectern of the Bible-reading in the candle-filled parlor, having forgot herself for a moment and crying, "Dear God, keep Emma away from those Fletchers, the skillful dealers in spells, those plotting and deceitful tongues . . . with dirty fronts." Her vivid specter had come up below my breath as it often did when I tried to think for myself. I sensed the turmoil in the tiny area of feeling which I always reserved for continuing fear. I was thinking of that list of truths which says that the world is what your grandmother says it is. "Beware of strange persons with gifts," she said, and she also said, "Not since Hannibal crossed the Delaware was there such great human deception as when your father, that bum, Egan Fletcher, came here and took your mother out under the pine tree. He'll come like a thief in the night and get *you* too; Willie Bee Fletcher, his mother, is a b-i-t-c-h!"

I thought it might be that moment!

I said, "Grandmother, don't." Then I said out loud so that Father could hear, "Oh, sir, let us go home, for the Fletchers, my relations, are wicked people who do not wash their fronts!"

The horror of the words echoed unpleasantly even to me, and Father, seeing the fear, pulled the Hudson to the berm.

He said, "Did you have a fight in your head?" gently.

He then looked decidedly hurt, almost as if he were resigned to something. But he said, "I want you to know, son, that your goddamned mother and your god-damned grandmother are liars."

With that he flew the car ahead without another word, leaving me only a small remnant of his now luminous presence. I had no words at all, and you could not hear the licking sound which I tried to make on account of my broken salivary glands. I stayed fearful all the way to the town of Vermen. I said nothing, though I wanted to. For example, I wanted to say that I did not agree with my grandmother anymore; I wanted to say, "What does *goddamn* mean?" The sound of breath drew me, for all its constancy, like the pleasant buzz of a barber's clippers. I was sustained in the upward movement of it.

Then what Father finally said was my Grandmother Fletcher's white bungalow rose up out of a wild poppy patch on a certain back road which Father found like a compass. That was what we came for, he said, and what you saw was mostly a quake of colors coming from the garden in the back.

There was an iron washpot steaming with laundry and its smell, and that was also what got your attention immediately. The vapor blew left in our direction when we got out of the Hudson, which means that it surrounded us like a fog.

The quite elderly lady whom father pointed out as Mrs. Willie Fletcher was sitting on the back porch on a green rocking chair. She was reading a newspaper and letting the pages fall out from her hands down under the rockers. There the great banner line had grown slowly, turned against the chair's movement, grinding out the word HI HIT HITLER, which I could read in those days.

Grandmother jumped up and said, "Oh, Joonie, you're here, and you've brung the boy too. Where's Emma, and where's the daughter?"

The wan face was uncautious altogether and she spoke out of a burst of exuberance accented by her yellow-gray hair and the heavy, indecorous rhinestone necklace which flashed about her neck like a chrome bumper. She was wearing an apron which she constantly wound about her hands as if to clean them. The dress was to her ankles and it was plain, and it seemed only finally to draw attention to the little face which jutted out of its apex, cut off from the rest of her by the jewelry glass. She was dipping snuff and the brown of it showed just delicately at the corners of her small mouth.

Father said, "Emma's stubborn . . ." Which was all he needed to say.

"Can I hug the child?" Grandmother Fletcher said, and Daddy Egan, a little distressed at the question, pushed her to me. Her eyes were a soft brown and sweet and you could smell her snuff. It was delicate and smooth the way she touched me, and I immediately placed the feeling at a far distance from Father's touch, nearer to his than Mother's or Grandmother's for its warmth, however.

They talked about Hitler and Grandmother said, "What, Joonie, if you have to go?" But the question did not move my father and he quickly enough had ushered us inside the house where we were faced with a lot of unmatching furniture. There were no vases anywhere, but the house had flowers. In the living room, where we finally sat, there was a picture of Hoover in his Masonic robes over the fireplace. Father leaned backward in a straight chair, and let his arms fall down beside him like a monkey's. Grandmother Fletcher kept playing with her apron, sending him secret signals, it seemed, which he always dismissed as though he did not want presently to be bothered.

At last you noticed that the far end of the parlor opened up on a room which had some beds in it. And there was also a curtain stretcher at one end which separated the beds. You got this smell, too, of perfume.

As though they were sideshow performers, my aunts emerged from the room with a theatric kind of finesse. Lovely as I had remembered them, they raced to Father and laughed in titters which went up high and gave you to believe their great happiness. With the same intensity which they had had in bringing Mother the scrapbook, they winked first toward me and then went on to give Father special gifts which they had concealed for the moment in their skirts: from Wexie, a new scrapbook; from Maggie, a pair of socks; and from Myra, a pair of drawers in a begonia print.

"Drawers?" he said. "Socks, a new scrapbook?" and they said, "O.K., now, Egan, put them on, you must put it all on!" They kissed him and pulled him up out of the chair, forming, on cue, a screen around him. When they stepped from before him, he was wearing the drawers and the socks and he said, "Ta-ta," like a fanfare, finally commencing to squat and direct the women into a game. They said they were playing baseball, and they ran the bases as Father kept squatting and pretended to be catching balls.

At length Aunt Wexie stood apart in her usual way and said, "Reckon the boy understands?" She said, "This is the game of baseball," to me, and Grandmother Willie Fletcher said, "For heaven's sakes, you'll scare the child to death. Joonie Fletcher, put on your clothes!"

Father dressed again while the women moved next to me on the cane-backed sofa and started to tickle me. They smiled wistfully and I laughed out loud, and though Grandmother Fletcher had also stopped them from that, I begged them silently to continue.

The afternoon, thereafter, seemed governed only by my aunts' looks of desperation. And I could tell, because they grew nervous once they had no more games to play, that some word or the other was making its way to getting said. Meanwhile Aunt Maggie was singing, "From the halls of Montezuma," and we went to the kitchen where we plopped back on our chairs and ate plums at the oilclothed table, and drank milk out of Mason jars. Still and all, the dark red of the women's carmine dresses swished a different tune, less moving, and more coarse, while, among other things, they called on me to do something that I knew or something that I liked. I said my speech from "Othello the Colored Man." I told them that my mother had taught it to me especially, that speech which goes, "I have loved not wisely but too well," and it was no sense thinking that they really listened. They laughed at the speech, but they patted my buttocks and kissed me afterward and put their fingers into my hair, saying, "What this boy needs is to learn to pitch and catch a few."

"Shhhh," Grandmother Willie Bee Fletcher said, looking at Father with an air of abandon. And then it was Aunt Wexie who, with everybody's encouragement, came over to my chair and took my hands warmly.

She looked exactly into my eyes and told me that there was a certain house which my father had had built for Mother and Elizabeth and me. It was a house, she said, quite as large as Grandfather's, and it was a place where we ought all to live now that Father was home for good. She twisted her face around to get approval from the others, though I neither understood her nor wished her to go on with it. For that moment I thought of how well Mother would have liked my speech from "Othello." I saw her gentle applause then, as if she were another specter who guarded me. I felt her arms around my waist, and I said, "Well, we have always lived with Grandmother and Grandfather DeWhit."

There had been no reaction but the one coming from Maggie, who suggested, "Why don't we just go down to that house anyway, and then maybe the boy can tell Emma about it and she will be convinced." It seemed that she sang her song over and over while Father drove us, but disappointedly, a short distance, through two forests and a cow pasture, to an enormous, new, and lovely house with six columns and a skylight. Out front, you found a statue of a man with a Bible in his hands, and then some forsythia and irises.

Father said, "I have been away, son, and this is what I have had made in the meantime. It is for you and your sister and your mother. What do you think?"

I looked at Aunt Wexie, who was smiling, and she told me quickly the whole story of how Mrs. Ella Mae DeWhit had run Daddy Egan off in the name of Jesus for being poor, and how, indeed, she had *not* been right to do so. "Then your daddy worked all this time and became the famous player of sports that he is. Here is the house he has built, and the one which his wife ought to come and live in. But no, she can't leave old Missus DeWhit . . ."

I said, "This is a very nice house," holding my father's hand tightly.

The laughter of those who heard me drew up like scorched silk. They held on to me and pointed, but I only watched Father. I danced with my aunts and smiled with them as they examined the contents of his house, though he himself watched the moments the way you watch a fly, knowing that there are fractions of seconds when you expect to be eluded. I was thinking how fine the visit had been, and I was thinking of Grandmother Fletcher who stood there stiff-legged and looked at me even though I was supposed to be concerned about other things. And you could have seen in her face a certain preoccupation which was very much the token of all the discovery, perhaps even of those feelings that finally have become everything that I know. Like a dress gusset, however, these feelings were hard to fit into the proper seams, and what hung out still was the great mystery of it all. Meantime, Grandmother Fletcher's smile was lovely. It was all lovely, and I looked back at her when we left the house in Vermen and thought that perhaps I *did* prefer her to Grandmother DeWhit, though, of course, she was only a w-h-o-r-e.

* 7 *

ON THE WAY HOME Father read the signposts out loud
because he thought it would please me. The imposing
face was dominated by his eyes which more than ever
seemed wide and engulfing. They stared ahead, moreover, with a display of caution, though he laughed at me
periodically and lifted his hand often to gesture me into
trying to read with him. Then he said, "I hope I can
talk your mother into living in this house which I have
built for her."

"It certainly is a great lot of furniture," I said.

Daddy Egan laughed once more and the concen-
tration in his face had carried until, arriving home, he
left me in the driveway and suggested that I play there
awhile.

I said, "You are going to tell Mother about the
house now, and I can see it."

And with that he had parked the Hudson and had waved to me and had gone inside where you immediately heard an absolute storm coming from the bedroom. Then Father left in a hurry, out into the car without a word, down the hill; his eyes were cast in an added soberness.

When I went to Mother, thereupon, and said, "There's this house which he has for us which I do not quite understand, but it's a nice house," she only cried out that she was betrayed again, and she did not make any sense. "He's even using the child," she said to the air; she dismissed me, adding, "Mama warned me what the child would learn in that place!"

With the cry going up like that and Grandmother soon arriving and joining in to add her own complaints, there had come many other questions as to the sense of it. I wandered the hallway and heard them almost rapt with their splendid fears, though Mother had quietened decidedly when Grandmother told her she ought to have him arrested for kidnaping.

What *I* did was go down the back hall to get away from the noise and inevitable questions and those tiny inner notes of their voices which sounded like an overworked vacuum cleaner. Then I was outside old Grandfather's back parlor thinking that I ought to go in there and talk to the old prophet about it. I could hear fewer funny noises coming from inside *there*, at least, and I stood quietly next to the door.

It was a quarter past and I knocked but no one

came. When I tried the knob it turned, and I was then standing in an immense darkened room strewn with plants, for one thing, and a lot of papers; a little fire in the fireplace. There was a chaise longue. There was another chair, center-room, which was spitting out its cotton insides.

And then you heard Grandfather's voice coming from the corner in a mumble. When I got past the old gray-colored chair, I could see that he knelt there on a broom handle, in front of an open Bible, naked and feeble.

He was saying:

> Joyous is he with whom
> God's word thou dost abide
> Sweet light of our eternal home
> To fleshly sense denied.

I was frightened, but as I had never seen anybody naked before, I was also curious. You had, besides, the quiet simple tone of his voice which reduced the fear; and then you had the prophet himself saying, "Well, come in now that you're here." He stood quickly and belched that he must be getting old: "Leaving the door unlocked to the children! What, maybe even to Ella Mae! Lock the door back," he said, and I did.

Then the old man said, "What can I do for you, son?"

I said, "I've never seen anybody naked like that."

"Well, now you have," he said, "but we won't consider it."

He sat down in the center chair and plopped me on his knee and I could feel the grind of his psoriasis scales under me. The great fleshy chest at once collapsed and went in again as he shuffled me around to get himself comfortable.

"I figured that I would have to get around to this sooner or later," he continued, "and you'll have to keep quiet about my prayers. I've got sins, you see. I have to make it up to the Infinite Ply."

I said, "Sins? What are your sins?"

He answered, "Never mind about that either." Grandfather said it showing his age.

I said, "O.K. — well — then," and I said it looking around the room, too, for whatever it was that made things dim. The shades were drawn and you got this funny stench coming up from the fireplace where he had put his dirty socks. The fire burned through wood that was charred and in its second ashes. Then you got the flashes of the only light besides the fire, a thin twenty-five-watt bulb which hung on a naked wire from the ceiling. Grandfather raised his hand in the magic for which he was famous, and you felt a wind; the Bible pages fluttered so that you knew he was a prophet again.

"Oh hell," he said, "now I do hope you won't say anything to your grandmother!"

He picked up the Bible and thumbed through it as though looking for a special passage. The edges of the onionskin pages were covered with notations in red ink. He added another and another.

I said, "Well, this man who is my father has come home and now there are many things which are new. They argue in the night and someone pounds on the table. They are doing love, I know, but they are very loud about it."

Grandfather smoothed his hair and laughed. He leaned forward and kissed my forehead, but coldly. He seemed completely preoccupied, though presently not with the Bible. His eyes flashed with a kind of doubt, at last, when he looked at me. Then I saw that he was looking at practically every part of my body. He started with my head and then went down. He shook his head about it.

"The point is, son, that you need your father and he is here now." Then the old gentleman would not look at me, but his voice remained soft and consoling. He stroked my hair and breathed on me; he closed his eyes as if he were having a fantasy.

"I have had that cotton mill to run," he said defensively, "and I have not had any time for you." Grandfather scratched his arms and seemed to be thinking even more deeply. Finally he looked at me. "You have been alone, and your mother has taught you. Your mother knows things, she knows about beauty. She many times used to be sitting beautifully under the pine tree where she read a book. Then Egan came to visit and your sister was born. Then your mother was not the same."

"I *know* about the pine tree," I said.

Grandfather coughed, the deep thought shifting to a

tiredness as though the moments were precious and he might any minute go to sleep.

"First I must tell you that there is God, who is called the Infinite Ply."

"*What*, sir?"

"The second thing is that I am your grandfather and I have this house here and my cotton mill which I am going to leave you."

"But I *know* that, sir."

"Yet the most important thing is that your father is home now."

Grandfather coughed again and studied his own left hand which made me entirely puzzled. He looked discomfited. He took his red pencil and jotted something onto the paper which he kept in the Bible. Indifferently he also pulled me to himself and held my face to his chest. The hairs which curled into my nose had the touch of feathers. They had the smell of sweat which lubricated our two fleshes. We adhered like tape, Grandfather and I, but then he pushed my face back and looked at me with saddened eyes.

"It is only important that you understand why your father is at home, and I would have told you sooner or later. Now I *have* to tell you that you must no longer listen to your mother about anything but what she knows. She is big on beauty, you see. Your father, on the other hand, knows the truth; he knows what duty is and he has been up there in the city of Washington doing his duty. Your mother has taught you about the

air, and those words from Shakespeare; she plays the
piano and all that; and all that is very good. But you
are a child, and now your father is here."

He struggled visibly to have the words correct, it
seemed, but when I told him that I did not understand,
he shivered. With former indifference his face stiffened
upward with finality, nonetheless. The dark mineral
smell of his body suggested a remoteness, though he
was brown like Father, and though his breath was similar as well.

"What I am saying," he said, "is that you must *go
with your father!*" He said it looking desperately toward the fireplace, and toward the photograph which
was there of Great-aunt Beans Duncan.

I did not ask him what that or anything else meant
because he removed his arms from me and he got up and
started to dress.

I said, "Is it different now?"

"No-no," he said.

Grandfather absent-mindedly said that he was only
tired. He slapped in his belt and patted his stomach.
He lit his pipe and in an apparent last-minute thought,
he once more sat down in the center chair. He put his
hands on my shoulders somewhat harshly.

"Now I told you that there was God," he said, "and
I told you I was going to leave you what I've got. I
really mean as well that you ought to do what I said
about your father."

The old man had his eyes heavenward and ran his

mouth around a little. He swallowed as if making a decision and then he breathed very slowly. He said, "I know what," and then he said, laughing with his indifference, "as your mother and grandmother don't know just how big *I* am on that beauty stuff, I'll show them and give you a riddle. I, myself, am not so bad at poetry either, and so let me think . . ."

He was suddenly happier for having brought me to look at him excitedly, and he mumbled a little. He studied and coughed, but smiled as well and wiped off the sweat at his forehead. He seemed to be at a game which he was winning in a subtle manner.

"Let's see," he said, "how's this: First, there are three columns — pillars, child, parapets, uh banisters — and on one is the word which your daddy likes, *duty*. On another is *beauty*, which is for your mother. And then the last is *truth*, which is what you will learn if you remember this riddle. Here — ha, ha, ha — is the riddle:

> One without U T Y
> Another less B U T Y
> The last missing T R U
> Together they spell th'Infinite Ply.

Ha, ha, ha, ha." Grandfather grunted, wildly looking toward the mantelpiece, toward the photograph of Aunt Beans, then toward the fireplace itself. He managed a deeper cough then and a wild sort of delight too; not for me, however, and I was frightened by it. I repeated the words because he insisted, though the old man also acknowledged my fear by saying, "Now come on, I'm trying to do it yours and your mother's way." He sucked on his fresh pipe and was pleasant again, ultimately slapping his stomach many more times, and then he said, "Now come again when you've got it. Be patient, and I promise to be around and help you understand."

He hobbled over and opened the door to dismiss me saying, "Come again, really," and at the last minute I said, "Grandfather, why were you naked like that?"

He said, "Couldn't you see that it was hot as hell in here?"

I stood in the hall outside for a while where I could hear the brown old clock ticking from Grandfather's parlor behind the closed door. I heard the dainty tick of Grandmother's clock down the hall as well. The chimes struck the half hour, one slightly before the other, and then I realized that Mother and Grandmother DeWhit had grown silent.

I relished my puzzled moments, remembering them mostly in connection with Father. Who is he, I said. Who is Father that he would have those answers that Grandfather said? Who was he that the very presence which finally confused even the words for him should have become so caught up with funny dispositions and with dark times?

I repeated Grandfather's riddle, presuming that he wanted me to laugh over it. But then I thought less of what he had advised than of what he had promised.

✻ 8 ✻

MEANTIME Father did not return for two days, and so
I practiced what I had learned best from him. I
breathed and I farted, though secretly in the foyer linen
closet where I also took out his letters from the napkin
Mother had hid them in again and tried to read all that
I could. There were certain words, for example, like
dear, Emma, hot, want, you, love, but I could not find
anything that I thought might spell *goddamn.* Then
I practiced remembering Grandfather's riddle.

Also in the meantime, both Mother and Grandmother
DeWhit were keeping a vigil at the front windows,
watching out there for the return of the Hudson automobile.

The latter boasted finally that "he deports himself like
a wart hog, and you could hardly miss him when he
arrives." Then her absolutely final remark, before
Mother openly disagreed, was "It's a shame, Emma, that

you ever trusted ———. I know what he wants, and I am glad you did not give it to him!"

Then shortly after lunch the day they obviously were expecting Father to return, Grandmother had emphatically prolonged the clock chore for the purpose of saying that she knew I had been to Vermen and that she knew I had been to the back parlor, "And what did you see over there, and did those women tell you anything? In short, did you betray your poor helpless Grandmother DeWhit with evil words?"

She looked down at me almost in the rhythm by which she wound the present clock and, on account of something she had eaten, her breath was like a sour dishrag.

I said, "Grandmother DeWhit, first, they did not *spell* anything at all, and, second, your breath stinks!"

She simply wailed out loud as she fled the room. She wailed that I had learned *that* over *there*. And she ran to Mother who was in the kitchen drinking coffee, where she cried, "You see what he has said to his own grandmother, Emma. Emma, he told his own grandmother that her breath stinks and he could only have learned such manners over *there!*" Grandmother ran to the toilet and you heard her trying to hide her gargle by running the water; she went upstairs to the sun porch afterward and sobbed loudly that Psalm which goes, "Oh how I do endure against these obstacles."

Mother, becoming perplexed, had got me to sit on the sofa in the parlor and her line of questioning went this

way: "Well, child, I suppose you don't want to tell
your mother what you did over there with your father
in Vermen?"

"No, ma'am," I said. But she said, "You'd better tell
me if you don't want to get paddled."

"We ate plums and drank milk; I said my speech
from 'Othello the Colored Man.'"

Mother's face lit over that. And I could feel a certain
pleasure at having said what I knew she wanted. For
the moment I was not even hostile toward her. But
Mother wore her look of sophistication, and the one
which indicated that she was ultimately only being nice.
She stared upward and whined to me in that way which
meant she had planned to have the last word anyhow.

I said, "Father is nice, and our relations in Vermen
are nice, and then there's Grandmother Willie Bee
Fletcher who is specially nice."

"Oh?" Mother said. She breathed so that you could
hear the bottom of her annoyed tone. Her eyes went
big and then small.

I felt vengeful. I said, "And I don't think that my
father went over there for any titty as Grandmother
says he does. I don't know what it is, but I don't think
he went for it. Father says that you and Grandmother
DeWhit are goddamned liars!"

The formerly pliant figure leaned back startled. Her
head got suddenly stiff and went up like a door latch.
Mother said nothing at all and grabbed me up under
her arm. She carried me immediately and furiously to

her upstairs bedroom which smelled like feet on the one hand and perfume on the other. She sat at her dresser and took the hairbrush to me. She hit me hard and long, and I cried.

"I have not raised you to talk to your mother like that!"

"But, Mama, what does it matter, as my relations are good and sweet. Grandmother DeWhit just doesn't know the truth."

"I am enough for you! Your father has tried to lure you away. You are not to say those words ever again. They are evil words and it is *his* fault that you are saying them. If I had an ounce more of strength I would beat you more for it!"

"Titty is *your* word, and Grandmother's word!"

Mother said it was not so, and she had leaned then, exhausted, against the table of the dresser where her body sprawled out over many tubes of cosmetics. The pink of her housedress sprayed out like a light and she was pretty. You could see her heart pumping in a little mound at the bosom of her gown.

She stopped her sobbing and got up from the dresser and came to me quietly. She was sniffing and trying to smile at last, and so I knew that she was not going to hit me anymore. She got down and smoothed off my tears the way father had done in the car, but it was not pleasant that she kissed my eyebrows and touched my throat. She pulled me into her arms then and held on.

She said, "I don't need him; I have you, child. Neither of us needs him, not you nor I."

But I was thinking what old Grandfather had said about Father, and I did not care what Mother was saying. About the bones of my arms I felt her hands still, though it was part my imagination. The quality of that movement, I mean that movement in my head which was like her touch from outside, was making me only think of how I wanted to tell her what I thought. The feeling was: Mama, I am not yours. Momentarily, I had as well made up other questions, and they were:

1) Why are words so important and why do they not mean what you want if Shakespeare or the Bible does not say them?
2) Why does the world move around in your mother's pink housedress?
3) What is titty?

For the moment Mother had also drawn me back to the dressing table where she combed her hair and pulled up the underpinnings of her housedress. She smiled and then tried to keep from crying again. She went and looked out the window.

"You don't know what it was like," she said. "Egan and I have loved each other, but you don't know what that means."

"He has built us a very special house."

"Never you mind about that."

"Why can't we go over there? Grandfather DeWhit said 'Go with your father.' "

Mother did not allow herself to be startled and she did not pursue my remark. Instead she took hold of me more tightly than before and she started to kiss me again. She ran her hands about my back, calling out, "Egan, Egan, years, acts, intimidations, oh God, oh Egan!"

She very tediously recited that part of the Song of Solomon which goes "into my mother's house and into the chamber of her who conceived me," though the final meaning which she assigned to her words had something to do with the poetry of it. At last Mother so helplessly looked at me that I kissed her as she wished and her bones then were like melting plastic. I had myself begun to cry for her when Father arrived downstairs calling out and looking tired.

When we went there he was in the parlor and he put down from his shoulders a red wagon which he carried and which seemed to contain several boxes of parcel post. Seeing Mother's careful hold on my arms, and seeing her tears, he did not say anything. She, on the other hand, did not ask. She kept her grip about me and restrained me from asking too. Finally she minimized his return absolutely by getting up a smile for Grandmother DeWhit, who just then entered and just then as well restrained herself from being curious.

At supper Father was, therefore, deathly quiet, though he watched me especially and smiled when Mother was not looking.

Elizabeth said, "Please pass the peas and pass the potatoes, pass some slaw, some of those seedless raisins, please."

"Another spot on the tablecloth," Grandmother said. "Oh that Nigger Ruth!"

"Such chablis," Mother said.

But then old Grandfather stood up at his place curiously. He flashed his wineglass up so that it made a shadow against the wall in the candlelight.

"A toast," he said, "a toast to you Egan, son. Take these apologies of mine. We are glad to have you home and now things will go right well. The boy's father is home and I can feel good about leaving him my house and my cotton mill. Here's to DeWhit Industries in Cotton in Kornelius-Above-the-South-Shoals too." He nodded coyly toward Grandmother but without particular deference. And she, pleased and displeased at the same time, lifted her glass submissively. It was not easy for anybody there to say anything, and so for the moment we had all watched Elizabeth about the business of gulping down her food. Her face was in moue like Grandmother's and she was singing quietly, between gulps, "Boo, de, bo, bo, dee, bop, beep."

Father winced. He looked at Grandmother DeWhit who put her head down. And Mother fidgeted more precisely until the meal was done. Completely in silence we dispersed, though Father had quickly pulled Mother aside with me. He called us into the parlor then and wheeled out the red wagon he had earlier brought. His own face was sweaty and he looked on the brink of anger without being necessarily urged on.

"Look here," he said with decision. "I've got the boy a baseball uniform. And here is a wagon for him to pull his equipment in. There's a bat, and here's a mitt and a ball."

He brought all of those things forth from the corner of the wagon and asked me, "Don't you want to put it all on, son?"

"Yes, sir," I responded.

But Mother said, "Oh, Egan, the child just can't go pushing that wagon around. People will think that he's dimwitted. Have you lost your mind!"

First she sighed and then tried to take the objects away from him. But Father put everything into my hands and forced me to push her away from them myself. With grave determination he also guarded me while I put on a uniform with the number 8, the cap, even a pair of shoes which clicked resoundingly on the marble foyer floor. Father's eyes were bright then, the face having let go its tautness as he rolled up his shirt-sleeves as if he were planning to work. He pulled me into a stiffened position and pushed my arms inward so that I was in a pitcher's stance.

"Look mean," he said, "look mean, and now say Bullshit."

"Oh my God," Mother cried; she wrung her hands frantically. She tried to move next to me and Father prevented it.

"Bullshit," I said, proudly, over and over, though Mother kept protesting loudly enough to have attracted Grandmother DeWhit from the kitchen. In she came, rumbling. Seeing me in the uniform, she cried, "Oh my God," as well, and then the two of them plowed their own heels together on the floor.

"I'll call the law," Grandmother said, and she came at him with her fingernails grinding. There was as well a distinct hiss in her voice as Father then tried to fend off the persistent fingernails. In a moment he had thrown her to the floor where she wailed like a child. She beat the floor too and said a Psalm.

"You've done it now," Mother cried.

"I've done nothing," he cried back. "The woman's a fool, and you're a fool. The two of you have ruined the girl, and now you want to do it to the boy!"

He put his hands to his face, and there was a moment of desperate silence in which Father at last stared at me pitifully. He scratched his head and then paced with his hands in his back pockets.

Grandmother DeWhit sobbed again. She stayed on the floor and patted her ankle and said it was broken. All along she moaned about the pine tree. The gist of it was that Father became the one who threw up his hands. The women finally were not even talking to him anymore and Mother was down there on the floor saying, "Does it hurt *here* or *here?*"

Much hurt, then Father drew up his nose a little and waved to me. He handed me the keys to Grandfather's car and quietly thumped me on the head. "I'll get a ride to Vermen with the drayman," he said, and then swiftly he was upstairs, returning with his suitcase half closed, his canvas brown coat thrown over his shoulder.

I went to Mother and cried for her to look at him. I said, "Father's going," and she did not listen to me. It was a matter of his having left silently and unnoticed. He shook my hand, and though I followed after him, he warned that I would get lost in the dark. He pushed me away and said that he had to think: he had to be alone, he said.

"Daddy Egan, Daddy Egan," I cried, watching the motion of his legs as he disappeared down Grandfather's hill, and I tried to see even beyond the distance which presently grew heightened on account of the quiet. Out front, the full darkness had taken him in, and I could only hear, finally, the river, down the other end of Grandfather's hill, lapping the bank; I felt the lights from the house eventually intrude on the darkness; then the moans from within came back too.

I sat on the fish pond ledge and no one came. The disappointment of it clamped on me with the splendid tightness of an embroidery hoop, though I eventually got up from there and went to the porch and up to the stair top. On the porch, beside the screen door, I found a wrinkled and soiled pair of Father's drawers which had dropped out of his badly packed suitcase in the rush.

I picked them up with an impulse to run down after him. I smelled them, and they had Father's brownness all right. But before I thought also to conceal them, Mother and Grandmother DeWhit came out looking for me. They drew me inside angrily and they made fast work of the baseball uniform. Mother took the drawers and groaned over them and shook them and said *uguggh*. First she pried my fingers from them, and then it took both of the women to get me out of the red wagon.

✻ 9 ✻

Now THE BEST PART of my grandfather's Memorial
Church was its balustrade. Surrounding the church on
all sides, this balustrade jutted out over the Church
Hill, and it jutted out over the river. For as long as I
could remember, Mother had allowed me to go there if
I did it in the early afternoon (when she could see me
from the front window) and watched in crossing the
Vermen road that no Chevrolets came and ran over me.
I liked to be there and put my hand over my eyes and
stare into the sun. Patterns came to my head, and I
could never control them, nor the colors which came
either.

With Father gone there was only just his absence
to dwell on, and I did not even have Mother's permission to go to the balustrade. I only lay there on my
own choice, many afternoons following, and there was

only this thought: will he ever come back? How can I go with him if he does not ever come back?

Mother was not caring so much about him for the moment. She nursed Grandmother's foot, with its fake ailment, because of course she could still wind the clocks. Once Mother did say, smiling just a little, "What if he *does* come back?" And the answer was, "Remember the pine tree!"

Mother watched the mail deliveries just the same.

And in the meantime I had found my baseball uniform and the red wagon in the linen closet. Once I put on the uniform secretly and went down to pull my wagon on the Vermen road. I put my feet in the stance which Father had taught me. I said *Bullshit* to the passing cars. I said it to Blazes Burnett, the drayman, when he passed us by with the mail.

I found Daddy Egan's drawers too, which Mother had washed and then stuffed into the uniform. There were many *what if's* in my head until I had undressed and saw that they were in fact too big; and then I wore them anyhow, especially when I thought of him on the balustrade where they perhaps seemed magic.

For the most part, all you could hear on that balustrade was Rachel Wainwright, the famous organist, inside, practicing Service Music. Her favorite was the "Meditation from *Thaïs*," and so she generally practiced that. And then most days, too, the Reverend Brendelle would be in there in his office to the side of the church, with the window open and the light on, practicing the next Sunday's sermon. For this he talked over to the corner where you knew that the devil was standing with a liver-colored pitchfork and a pair of sunglasses. He was also picking his teeth.

I put up two fingers to the sun. I imagined the darkness to which my feeling descended. To my stomach and then up to my head. The sun had played its colors on the insides of my eyes and they changed outside my control.

Father was in the colors, I imagined, but he came and went with them too: his face recognizable for a moment, crystalline like a lemon drop on meringue, but then gone.

Then I put my arm up to the sun so that the hairs on my wrist made a forest. The sun through the forest thereafter gave me Daddy Egan again. The face came forward, but just as soon as I thought myself able to touch it through the forest of my arm, it changed to a face that I did not know. It changed to the face of the Reverend Austin Brendelle and he was standing over me saying, "Oh it's Robert DeWhit's boy again, and I guess you're here once more staring idly into the air."

I said, "I don't know what idly means, and I am not my grandfather's; I am . . ."

He said, "Excuse me then," and his cotton yellow face stretched tightly over its bones like curtains on a stretcher. He had a little white chalk substance on his lips that kept coming and going.

"I have been meaning to talk to you about your

father," he said, "as there are certain things I should like to know; for example, is it true that he threatened your grandmother with a rifle, then beat her within an inch of her life, and cast her roughly onto the marble floor of your grandfather's foyer?"

"My grandmother is a goddamned liar," I said.

The Reverend Brendelle mourned and looked in many directions. He said, "Those are athaletic words, child, and you learned them from your father, the player of sports, and you should not say them. They are evil and I should turn my back on them and go away."

Then the Reverend cleared his throat and told me that was not what he wanted to talk about. Moreover, he said, "Those are not words for a Christian child and you should stop them as I have said." He raised his triangular eyebrows and stared out over the river which silently begged its way down to the reservoir at Grandfather's mill. I did not listen to him then, and Daddy Egan's face came and went again above his words. I was waving my hands back and forth so that the light was coming in and out with the movement. It was a pleasant sensation, then to have felt the warmth in my own patterns. It was as if I had been given control over the light, too, and it was as if Father had done it. Inside my clothes, in the vacuum between the clothing and my skin, I felt myself rise up. Lifted was the best word because it was not a sensation really of floating. It was cold as well. And the sensation lasted only just a moment. Then I thought it a sort of magic which seemed even to have blanched the sun and seemed to have loosened in a funny way like a wrinkled cloth being pressed.

The sudden courage of my feeling made me feel like telling the Reverend to hush up.

He was saying, "Well, as for the spiritual sense, your father, the athalete, has a lot to learn. Does he render to God and do as he *must?*"

"Grandmother was there," I said, "wailing, and she came in at him with her fingernails. Then he did what he must and put her on the floor. If that is the spiritual sense, then my father does it."

Reverend Brendelle threw up his hands and turned his back. He told me that there were certain things which he must take up with my mother about my condition and he was quiet in an annoying fashion. He thrust one hand under the pit of his other arm, touched his forefinger quickly to his lip. He went away.

I lay on my back again with my knees up. I put my foot up to shade the sun so that I saw the butt of a spade with a halo. Once again I saw Father and I knew that he had been driven away and I began to feel that I should at least have kicked Grandmother a few times to help him. I sensed a deep chill around the church. At last the chill rested in my head. I felt my insides move slowly. It was a sudden largeness of bone, a growing feeling in the stomach and in the flesh of my thighs with the pleasantness of a yawn. And it was as if the trunk of my body rose above the rest of me. Finally there was a quick, divisive sensation that separated my thoughts from my body too, coming from nowhere, which endured only in effect.

Below me and to the left, you could see Grandfather's mill only distant a couple of hundred yards, and there you could see that Grandfather himself was standing out to the right of it. Great-aunt Beans Duncan was with him and the two of them were raising their arms in the air frantically. It was not an argument, I thought; it was rather a kind of pleading by which the two of them seemed to be questioning each other. They were moving eventually as if in search of something as well. At last I could see that they were upset with whatever they searched for. And they walked therefore upon the path which went to the back of the mill and out into the Brush Pile which lay beyond.

I came out of my own thoughts. I stood and scratched at the insides of my father's drawers, and then I saw that at the far end of the Brush Pile, very near the river and up from the reservoir, my sister and Clyde Duncan were sitting and holding hands as I had seen them before in the nandin bush. They had been unaware altogether of the pursuit which Grandfather and Beans Duncan were making, and Elizabeth was giggling. Clyde's dark tanned face had got about it a wistful look that suggested he was having fine thoughts. He was smoothing back his hair with his other hand, and then he started to play with the beads which Elizabeth had around her neck.

When Grandfather and Great-aunt Beans arrived
there they had done so in visible anger. Beans was
throwing up her arms. She hit Clyde, and Grandfather
grabbed Elizabeth by the arm and stared at her. There
was a space between him and her, a space, as well, between Grandfather and Great-aunt Beans. They were
looking tortured the way Mother looked when she
paced the floor and called out for Daddy Egan.

I had not understood any of it, and I was inclined to
laugh first at the way Elizabeth finally looked with her
face all offended and her head up high. Clyde was
scratching his groin and fidgeting, which was the second
funny thing. But with a degree of apparent resignation,
they left, Grandfather and Elizabeth in one direction,
and Beans and Clyde in another.

What I recalled was my sister's special words about
doing love; and I recalled that she had said of Clyde,
"Oh how he does move my soul." She had said it
twisting those same beads which she said he had given
her as a token of his "necessity." It struck me that
Elizabeth and Clyde had touched the way Mother and
Father did. But I had never seen Grandmother and
Grandfather touch that way.

Lying on the balustrade, I had lost the earlier feeling
of being cold. That Father was gone returned as the
prevailing awareness, and then old Grandfather's words
came up above it all faintly as if to warn that the confusion had only just begun. His riddle, which I could
only remember in its words, became momentarily the
special secret token, I think, of certain impulses which

I could not fathom at all. Otherwise I was left for a time with a nervous stomach, although there was a sudden upward motion which then came over me. It ran deeply to my thighs, and especially to the seat of my trousers, where I seemed wet.

✳ 10 ✳

NIGGER RUTH THE PROPHETESS had never much come
to Grandfather's house but to wash clothes and dishes.
She lived in a shack in the Brush Pile on the Mill Hill
beyond Great-aunt Beans's house. You could not see it
from the Memorial Church.

The word was that Elizabeth had got used to going
down there to Ruth's where she learned how to put on
makeup and drink Pepsi-Cola from Ruth's daughters,
Mascara, Acacia, and Turtledove. But neither Mother
nor Grandmother DeWhit had ever caught her at those
sins.

Nigger Ruth's real name was Mrs. Jobson in those
days, and Grandmother DeWhit had that habit of complaining about her work, but she also had spent more
than a few afternoons listening to the sweet yellow
woman say that the world was in a rotten mess. Grand-

mother agreed, but more often than not Nigger Ruth spoke as well about the fit of Grandmother's dress instead, and sometimes you could hear her say, "Ella Mae, it just ain't like it used to be, is it?" To that statement Grandmother would also nod her approval.

The point is that the real Nigger Ruth was truly a prophetess as everyone said. And Grandmother DeWhit was neither above asking questions like "Will I survive the night?" nor above saying, "I'll give you fifty cents if you promise that Emma won't leave me."

The question had got Ruth to answer with a little sigh, "My powers ain't over life nor death, they is over comings and goings and over love affairs. As for Emma's leaving you, it ain't a fair question!"

On the balustrade I was thinking that Nigger Ruth ought therefore to be the one to help me with my questions about Father. Things were not going well, and time had only slowed down both my colors and the pictures I had wished to conjure up. I was only customarily bewildered by former expectations. The sun hid, but with a residue of its earlier power.

Then, "Pssst" came a sudden quiet voice from the other side of the balustrade. There on the climb of the Church Hill, crawling in the tiger flowers which grew wild, was that person named Tolly Butterworth. I only knew him from church on Sundays when he had likely been the one who stared at me most when we DeWhits exited, or else he was the one who raked leaves for Grandmother. Elizabeth always said that he was the one in high school whose sisters they asked about also, and they said, "How much is Butterworth?"

The adolescent figure who finally came up beside me smelled like Clorox and he had skin like a horse's which I had never noticed because I had not ever been up close. If you added up his smell, and the way he looked, then, you might have been afraid, but then he said, "I know *you*, and I know that your old silly grandmother is crazy as a loon. But I know that your daddy, Egan Fletcher, ain't."

He was chewing on a piece of brush straw. His clothes were soiled from the climb which he had made up the Church Hill. He looked out over the river then and toward Grandfather's house, then toward the Mill Hill which was presently animated by the sound of machinery.

"Look at all of that," he said, "and your granddaddy owns every piece. That don't change it, though, that your grandmother is crazy as a loon, which everybody knows. They know that your mama, Emma Ruth Fletcher, has also got problems with her bottom parts and they know that your sister is dimwitted."

"None of it is so," I said, "but it *is* true that my mother has some problem."

"I know where your daddy is."

"Where, where!"

And Tolly Butterworth won me to his way of thinking altogether. First, he said that Father had gone off to Washington where he was busy at the game of base-

ball once again. Tolly said that the whole world knew
how he had come to Kornelius to get his wife back and
how she would not go with him on account of her
bottom parts. Then he said that for fifty cents he could
take me down to Nigger Ruth's where, if I liked, I could
get all the information I wanted.

I said, "I don't have fifty cents," and he said, "Well,
you can make it an IOU." Explaining what that meant,
he put his face into a growl then and he suggested that
the two of us ought to talk awhile. He assured me, first
of all, that he had only my interests at heart, and then
he said that he had admired me for a long time and was
waiting for a chance to tell me what I ought to know.
As for what he meant by that, he grew silent when
asked, and tilted his head willy-nilly to suggest that he
would let me know soon enough.

That time Tolly had explained his own ambitions
as well, and he said that my part of it had to do
with finances. He said that someday he wanted to go
to Brazil where you could still get a slave for $14.95.
He would have thirty-five of them, he claimed, and he
would open a plantation which would send the cotton
back to Grandfather's mill in Kornelius, where I would
then be the boss.

"There are other things too, and I will tell you sooner
or later," he said, "but for now, we ought to get ourselves off to Nigger Ruth's if you want to find out
the truth about your daddy."

Tolly hesitated over my emergent confusion, but he

managed an encouraging laugh. Then he was off, calling to me to follow him into the Brush Pile. He conceded no other questions either, though with a sudden exuberance he finally brought me to Nigger Ruth's house and said, "There it is."

"And here I is," she said, arriving at the door in the blue apron with which I was familiar.

"Nigger Ruth, Nigger Ruth," Tolly said, "we are here for some prophecy. Tell this boy about his mama and then tell him about his daddy."

But Ruth said, "What in the world is you doing here with Robert DeWhit's grandson?" And she said, "Now you boys go on and you boys behave yourselves."

The yellow woman shook her head while we waited disappointedly. She knew it and of course she turned to acknowledge what seemed more than a prophetical understanding. Ruth went deliberately to me as well and she put her hand on my head in a special manner. Her smile, like Aunt Wexie's, had but a single intensity, the wistful look about her also a sort of encouragement, which, for the moment, merely intensified my wishes.

But she said, "Well, child, sooner or later it's going to be your problem too, ain't it."

Mrs. Jobson patted my shoulders warmly. She also said, "Don't worry about your mama and daddy. They used to come here in the old days when I was their original encouragement, and that's all I have to say. I knows, for instance, that they loves one another." She went on cautiously to say that Father would be back, adding softly that certain questions she knew would have to be reckoned with. "It's a matter of time, too," she said. For that she also nodded severely and did not say anything more. She waved us off then, as though she did not want to talk about what had suddenly come to mind.

Meantime, Tolly Butterworth promised that he would help me learn the game of baseball properly. He also promised a baseball team when the time came. Otherwise he said, "There's something else I want to tell you for now, and so follow me."

In a short time he had taken me down by the mill reservoir where there was a headward gully full of water. He said, "Here we'll go swimming," and he undressed himself very nearly in a single breath.

He said, "Now you undress and come on in the water hole because no boy your age ought not to know certain things and one of them is how to swim."

I undressed myself by his prescription until he had seen my great white drawers. I told him that they were my father's drawers, and he laughed out loud and said, "Well even if you can wear your daddy's famous drawers, I've got something that you haven't."

Tolly faced me with his body caught in the sunlight and he spread out the little dark patch of hair about his groin and said, "You see?"

I said, "No?" but he had looked at me as if I ought to have got some point or the other, ultimately annoyed that I had not responded with more astonishment. Then he pulled me into the water and got me to float and I trusted him. He splattered the water in my face as well. He drew a map of Brazil in the air and then told me exactly the place where he would put his slave plantation.

When it was done and we were dressed, Tolly and I sat on the edge of the headward gully where pink wild poppies grew. He was pulling up the poppies and telling me that he had wanted to be my friend for a long time. He said, "I knew that you didn't have anybody up there in the house, and I knew that your grandmother and mother were crazy as loons." He said it while he threw a mass of the flowers into the air and then he took hold of me the way Elizabeth often did. He lay on my back and forced me to fight him, and, at length, after the scuffle, he had sat back against the bank and undid his trousers and took it out and said, "You see what you've done, don't you? You see that you've made it hard."

I said, "Well, we must get the doctor quick."

But Tolly grimaced at me. He shook his head and told me that I did not know *anything*. You could see the disappointment which came on his face, and Tolly admitted that he had not been able to teach me the first lesson he thought I ought to know. Finally, he said that here was what I ought to remember about what he had done for me:

Pecker is what it is which gets hard if you play with it
Poon is what you play with it for
Hump is the name of the game

I wanted only to remember that Nigger Ruth told me I would see Father again. Tolly said it too, though even then he was annoyed that first things had not been first.

Ultimately he only laughed out loud and suggested that I keep it all to myself if I ever wanted to see him again.

I said, "Yes, I will," and, puzzled, I watched him button up his trousers. He led me back to the Church Hill where it had almost got dark and where I felt that my father's drawers had suddenly been more important than ever. I was mostly content for the moment, but I was also aware that my friend had laughed at me again and looked into the sky with his head up, perhaps vainly.

* 11 *

At home Mother was washing coffee cups at the kitchen sink and watching for the mail, and she knew immediately that I had been with Tolly Butterworth for she said, "I saw you from the window talking to that child of darkness down at the church, and I want to know what he was telling you."

"Nothing," I said.

"Well then, where have you been all this time? I saw you leave the church with him, and I saw you return. Where have you been, child?"

"Well, uh Tolly Butterworth and I went off to Nigger Ruth's shack in the Brush Pile for some prophecy. I asked her about my father and where was he. That was all it was, and she said that you and father used to . . ."

Mother stooped from the sink. She was not exactly

annoyed, or at least she stopped that expression which had suggested anger and changed to a troll mouth which was a little softer. Then she continued, "I am enough for you, child. I truly am, and I don't see why you have to go off looking for Egan Fletcher. Do you not love your mother?" she whispered, and I said, "Yes," though I also told her that I was not sure what it felt like. I told her that I liked having a friend and she only winced to say that I had better watch out with him. I had not understood that, and I did not ask her to explain.

Mother let me go that time, mostly because Grandmother had come in with her fake limp complaining that Grandfather had just made up another rhyme about her and Great-aunt Beans; she said, "And I don't know what to do, Emma. He's old and feeble, but he has a filthy mouth." They were talking on and I went to the linen closet in the foyer where the air smelled of the clean bed sheets that Ruth had finished ironing. The cool smell was intoxicating and so was the light musty odor at the bottom of the Kirby vacuum cleaner that Grandmother kept there. I put my nose into it and I smelled the collection of scents which somehow had my grandfather's entire house in it. The thin little residual threads of lint attached to the bottom seemed as well to have been a careful pattern of all the house's colors.

Then, in the foyer outside, the Reverend and Mrs. Austin Brendelle arrived for a *visitation*, they called it, and I could hear them commencing with that prayer which goes, "Oh God in heaven save us all from the devil," after which Mrs. Brendelle held Mother in her arms and cried just a little for the ritual's sake. Grandmother DeWhit had arrived soon enough as well, carrying the best tea service which she put down momentarily in order to exchange the same greeting. All bleary-eyed they went down into the parlor, and I, from my sanctuary, unseen, had cracked the door a little more for a better view.

The customary light of the afternoon gathered there; like nearby secret passages, however, the shadows inside the closet had drawn me down inside themselves. The words of Grandfather's riddle seemed the apt thing to consider though they remained meaningless; and I thought that I had forgotten to ask Nigger Ruth about them. I felt, also, the sober pressure of Tolly Butterworth on my back. The deep and liquid motion of my feelings had then but recalled Mother's own notion about words, and this is what I said to myself: why can I not think of the right way to say all of this? Why can I not ask it when the time comes?

The thought was itself like the sun on the church balustrade. It came and went against the slow drone of the Reverend's voice outside, though aloft even with those unpleasant remarks I began to feel a new moment of intensity. I thought that I felt the air and the light where there were also sounds. Like my own hands, the air and the light moved and the sounds moved. I could feel Tolly Butterworth moving in such flashes as if he were also a kind of light. Then there was Father whose face was *there* and then *not there*.

The closet held me securely. It consoled me. Other objects there, though reflecting Grandmother's choices, were not sometimes ugly like her; and I wondered why. You had all the spotless and shining service things, the crystal stemware with gold edges, and goblets and napkins with the monogram RSD. A paper, attached to a board, hung in triplicate from a masonry nail, and I could read it without knowing how, simply because the letters stood for something more than the words which lay behind them. In the same manner as the clock schedule, they revealed THE CONTENTS OF PLATE AND HOUSEHOLD ITEMS OF ROBERT S DEWHIT AND FAMILY FROM THE PEN OF MRS ELLA MAE DEWHIT:

17 Nipponeze glass rose bud vases
17 island glass cupps
17 buillyon cupps
31 linentable clothes (with Mr. DeWhits name) 100 matching napkins
51 downstairs towels (without Mr DeWhits name)
 1 entire set of crystol, 31 wine glasses, 31 water goblettes, 1 punche bole, 30 punche cupps, 31 shirebet glasses and prafay with golden edge each
   more assorted prafay glasses in the above desine (that is with the golden edge)
 1 entire set of crystol with a golden edge too and with Mr Robert DeWhits name pressed on it of the same number as above

Outside, the Reverend at last was sitting with his wife on the Duncan Phyfe sofa, his hand on her elbow, before Mother, who was coughing. She smiled mechanically at the Mrs. who returned the smile out a whisper veil, off the edge of a wine-colored hat with a quill.

"My, your children are so well behaved," Mrs. Brendelle said.

"I know," Mother said, "and you are exactly right."

I was counting out the napkins with the monogram and listening to them go by with a ventilating slap. They smelled of cedar, thirty-one of them exactly.

The Reverend said, "And you have done so well as to have these children adept at vast numbers of occupations. The young *Miss* Fletcher does domestic fare, and I understand that the children know their Longfellow and their Cervantes."

"Oh, yes, and the boy may even be a poet," Mother said.

The Reverend grimaced and gulped and he told Mother, whisperingly, what he had come to tell her: that her younger child was inclined to use that athaletic language that he had learned from his father.

Mother returned, "Oh?" but she did not pursue it, and the Reverend rolled his eyes and said, "Very well, but when *I* hear words like that I can only turn my back on them."

In the room Mother and Grandmother DeWhit came and went, refilling the silver teapot with the contents of a crockery urn which they brought just as far as the dining room sideboard so as not to be seen with it. Taking turns they said, "More tea, Reverend?"

He said, "Well, very well, just so long as it is not Pepsi-Cola, ha ha."

Then the Reverend looked solemn and extended his

hands outward in a gesture of giving. He asked after Grandfather. "I know that the poor man works very hard. I know, for instance, that the mill is killing him. The church and the town are more than grateful. Thirty-five years," he said, staring coldly around the room, "thirty-five years," slowly, as if it had come out of constipation.

I counted out that number on my fingers and toes, on my ears and nose, and eyes, and the shoelaces in my sneakers: four more than the number of table napkins with the monogram. I opened the closet door a little wider and I saw Grandmother DeWhit, holding her head very proudly, go away to the kitchen to wash the silver teapot.

The late afternoon by then had adjusted itself further to the proper weight for penetrating the parlor's great velvet curtains. Mrs. Violet Brendelle adjusted the quill on her hat, too, which was the customary signal that it was time for the *visitation* to have ended. "Pray against sins," they warned, "for even the most righteous among us may fall, even Brother DeWhit would warn us from time to time of backsliding. You see, don't you?"

Mother answered, "Yes," faintly. And she said, "Oh we never forget our prayers in this house, as you know." She got down on her knees with the Reverend and Mrs. Brendelle for the benediction. Answering the words of the ritual, she nonetheless had a queer little drum in her voice as she said Amen. At last the Reverend said, "May the thoughts of our hearts be acceptable," and so forth.

Thereupon, uncertainly and feverishly, Grandmother DeWhit reappeared at the dining room doorway and her face was drawn as white as the color of wash. She could barely stand, and she was groaning with words that seemed unutterable for her. She was simple about it, however, and then she was intense as always, though finally she bellowed with her mouth open wide and in agony, "Robert, my Robert, is dead on the tree stump in the backyard. Oh, Jesus-God, he is right dead and I am sure. He doesn't breathe, Emma; he looks into the air and he is dead."

"Are you sure of this," the Reverend said as Grandmother fell limp and leaned on a wall. She yelled, "Go quickly to the stump which is up from the chicken house. He went there, I am sure, to feed the chickens and he died. Go see if he isn't dead. He tried to feed the chickens, but he is dead!"

Mother started an angular noise on the letter E. She called out and ran from the room accompanied by the spectral Reverend and his wife. They chanted their advice like a litany and said, "Lord have mercy," together, and then Mrs. Brendelle said, "Well, maybe Brother DeWhit is only sleeping."

There is no better way to put it than simply to say that old Grandfather *was* out there on the tree stump. As for the fittingness of it, there was no better place of course, but the question was how to determine exactly what he was dead of or how he had died. And that was the Reverend's worry. They stood around as

Grandmother jumped up and down. She screamed and bellowed more and got down there on top of the tree stump with him like a hen on an egg. She was kissing him and letting his hair fall down. She held on to Mother's hand and Mother also screamed so that the nurses came and two ambulances. The law came. All together they screamed so that they were out of control. Then Aunt Beans came and Uncle Fred, who was scratching his arse and looking down at him over a cigarette. He said, "Yes, he's dead," and soon everyone else said it too — he's dead — until the Reverend got his prayer book.

I watched it all from the back porch where, for the moment, I held my sister's hand. Elizabeth had come up from riding and she did not say anything and finally went out there to help. She did not say, "This is the end of him," or anything like that.

As the old prophet had told me that he would show me the solution to his famous riddle, I could only presume that they all had been very mistaken, and so I went back to the closet and listened as Mother went off crying with Grandmother DeWhit. They all went off crying, and I was alone in my grandfather's old house. I leaned back against the Kirby vacuum and took off everything but Father's drawers. I brought down my mother's secret scrapbook compacted among the table napkins. I thumbed once more through Daddy Egan's letters, looking to see if there had been other words there which I knew. As there were none, and as the house was so very silent, I fell asleep with a certain powerless sensation, albeit in the process I let the monogrammed napkins which rested on top of the scrapbook go by in a shuffle before me one by one: like a deck of cards: RSDRSDRSDRSDRSDRSDRSD RSDRSDRSDRSD.

✳ 12 ✳

W<small>HEN</small> M<small>OTHER</small> <small>FOUND</small> <small>ME</small> asleep in the closet she had not had time to worry about it. She moaned from the center of her face, and shook her head midst the other sighs. "Well, your dear grandfather has gone over to the other side." And then, the next morning when she had got everything organized well enough, she told me that I really ought to cry over his death, especially since he had left me his money.

I responded that I did not quite understand any of that, nor what it meant to be dead, and she said, "Of course you don't, but it's the principle of the thing — and there you were asleep in the closet in your father's drawers. What kind of a child are you anyhow?" For the time being, she kissed me sorrowfully and went away.

Grandmother DeWhit, on the other hand, was staring

with a faraway look, even though she also, from time to time, sat quietly and wept beside the armory which contained the Sacred Bolts of Grandfather's first fabrics. She nursed the cloth for the first few days, and then she put it back and took the key to the old man's back parlor. Going in there, she carried everything out single-handedly (before even the lawyers could get to it) to the tree stump in the backyard, where she burned it with kerosene. You could see her crying more, and then laughing intermittently, until even the Bible with its red-lined margins had turned to charcoal. For days afterward, even up to funeral time, the stump smoldered on and she went out there to see it. Grandmother said, "Well, child, I suppose now we must carry on with God's help."

But finally she also seemed less happy with God. For one thing, she stopped the Bible readings and became intently occupied with the workings of DeWhit Industries. At least for the moment, Grandmother called in Great-uncle Fred Duncan, the overseer, and told him to make sure the niggers did not run wild. She had never trusted Uncle Fred anymore than Aunt Beans, and for a time you might have thought that she was taking her final revenge against her sister.

She said, "I know that Robert was bound to have left Beans money, but not much. I don't want it to be much."

She told this to Uncle Fred out beside the woodshed, and he responded that he thought the Duncans were as deserving as anybody else, seeing as how . . . but he did not finish because Grandmother shushed him. Accordingly, she soon emerged angrily from her own bedroom with a list of what was what, she allowed, and she read it first to Fred, and then to everyone who would listen. It was called THE DISPOSITION OF GOODS OF ROBERT DEWHIT ACCORDING TO HIS WIFE ELLA MAE DEWHIT WHO IS THE ONLY ONE WHO OUGHT TO KNOW:

Property, general:	a white house and 50 acres of land above a cotton mill with 150 employees mostly niggers; a gray Hudson modeled before 1940; 35 chickens and the propers of the chicken house, as well as 5 suits of clothes with shirts; and black galoshers not fit to keep
Bank assests:	tew hundred thousand dollars left to the boy
Property laterly discovered where he hid it:	a typing machine and some sheets of yellow typing paper, 30 North American Savings Bonds
	three boxes of instraments for prevention of venerial disease
Property privately discovered	one hobnail vase, one electrick fan, one key chain, one whet stone, one copy of a Bible with red marks in it, one stack of chicken feed,
	one belt buckel engraved love Beans

Bequeaths   Everything else to Mrs Ella Mae
                         DeWhit wife of Robert DeWhit

                         except a mere 14,000 dollars to Beans
                         Duncan and that is all

Meantime the funeral was being prepared according
to the proper standards; and meantime Elizabeth came
to me at the fish pond saying, "Well, Grandfather is dead
and I am going to cry. I will take you over there to the
chicken house so that you can watch if you don't inter-
fere. You will see how I truly miss him."

I said, "I saw you and Clyde Duncan down there by
the river, and I saw Grandfather nearly paddle you
home. I know you didn't really care for him."

"You little demon," she said, going limp. And while
Elizabeth was there moaning under a pecan tree presently strewn with chicken feathers, they came and took
us to the Memorial Church in a Jonesgay Mortuary
limousine with a gold hood ornament. There, Grandmother DeWhit proclaimed immediately, "Well, here
they come, the flute players and the mourners just as in
Jesus's time. This is the crowd that he took the lash
to." She especially seemed to have in mind Grandmother Fletcher and my three aunts, who stood un-
attended and awkward but were not like all the rest of
the people who said it was a hasty death and a tragic
one. The greatest of the mourners occupied the
front seats, however, Grandfather DeWhit's own relations from the town of Floyd, whom we had only seen

on brief occasions such as other funerals or when once in a while they would have come to the house in Kornelius for the sake of mysteriously tormenting Grandmother DeWhit: they were our Cousin Dannie, and Grandfather's sister, Aunt Toy Trilby Slide, and his brother, Uncle Jericho Valeu DeWhit. They all were crying while Rachel Wainwright played the "Meditation from *Thaïs*."

Himself weeping, the Reverend Brendelle began by standing up in front of the flowers above the box which was dressed in three large chrysanthemums (to represent the Trinity, Grandmother insisted); there were thirty-five coils of baby's-breath from the Chamber of Commerce, and Aunt Beans had also placed there a sprig of honeysuckle.

Great-uncle Fred, among the commentators, whispered that "there is no goddamned resurrection and this is a lot of foolishness." He moved his place nearer to Mother with a grimace. He folded his arms and shook his head.

At last the Reverend shook his own head and said, "I will begin the eulogy now, but first is there anybody with an unsolicited testimonial?" By then unbearably distressed by whatever bothered him, Uncle Fred shot up in his place and made his speech about the resurrection, though he did not use the former words. At length, looking at Aunt Beans and then at Grandmother with an angry burst of courage, he went on: "There's no sense pretending that old Bob DeWhit didn't play around and the whole town knows that. Now I feel we ought to talk about it and I feel we ought to discuss what is going to happen to the cotton mill. He's dead, but we're alive."

Grandmother DeWhit stood up.

"You watch what you say, Fred Duncan, and as for the money, I have already told you about that." She drew from her purse the paper upon which her plan had been written. She pointed to it and waved it in the air and everybody nodded truly, even the Reverend Brendelle, who finally said, "Fred Duncan, please sit down or else leave, as this is a funeral and not a Chamber of Commerce meeting."

Then you had it that they sang six verses of "The Sweet Bye and Bye" and two of "Beulah Land," which gave Rachel Wainwright trouble in the pedal. Great-aunt Beans led, and she cried stalwartly, better altogether than Grandmother DeWhit, who seemed only content that the Reverend had prevented Uncle Fred's further testimony.

The Reverend himself had preached at last on what favor must have been shown when a man lived more than threescore years, and he praised such favor, allowing it to Grandfather DeWhit in great abundance. The earthly prison, he said, was done after all those years of faithful service, and blessed Brother DeWhit, owner of DeWhit Industries, had *gone to the throne alone.*

From within the box, where he seemed to rest quite

comfortably on the billowed pillow, old Grandfather only gave instructions to ignore the show. I knew he was saying it to me because I was the only one who really looked at *him*. His whitened face, as a sign, was no surprise at all, the only difference between then and other times being the absence of sweat. There was as well, I saw, that great pulse of command which remained as always, borne with mere half interest, and with assured preoccupation over other matters. I thought it magic that perhaps he pondered the proper Bible verse, or maybe his own funny riddle.

Finally the Reverend bowed and called us together around the box where you could hear the cries of Great-aunt Beans suddenly get louder. In fact, Grandmother DeWhit and she had seemed at last to grow friendly again, even in their sorrow, and so they cried together for the first time in quite a while.

The Reverend went around to everybody and shook hands. He seemed to be everywhere at once.

Aunt Maggie and Aunt Myra and Aunt Wexie, with Grandmother Willie Bee Fletcher, crowded up for a single moment in the background, and so did Nigger Ruth. Each of them seemed led to touch Mother with a single finger and they nodded. They looked heavenward, all of them, and then they were gone.

Great-aunt Beans at last kissed the pall too, and while everybody else occupied himself with the final cries, I got up there quite alone with him myself. I was afforded all the time I needed to say, "Stop me if I get any of it wrong: there is duty and beauty and truth?"

I was certain that he nodded to me.

While the box was, thereafter, carried out and we followed, the Reverend Brendelle said "Wie geht's." I noticed all the relations' responses of sorrow, and I saw that Tolly Butterworth was there. I had got to notice that the Reverend Brendelle's triangular head towered above everybody else's also. But then my secret wish was that Daddy Egan had been there, for his head would have been even higher than that.

✳ 13 ✳

AFTER THE FUNERAL, the remaining relatives sat in the parlor and spoke of Grandfather's ability to conjugate the verb *duco* in the past periphrastic. It was Dannie, his clubfooted cousin from the town of Floyd, who made that assertion while her brother, consequently my relation too, Great-uncle Jericho Valeu DeWhit, propped himself on the arm of the chair next to her and ate popcorn from a faded yellow butter-stained paper bag which he eventually, without Mother's notice, threw empty behind the cloth armory.

This Cousin Dannie, painted up like Bernhardt in the role of Queen Elizabeth, explained a number of things including the circumstance of her clubfoot, upon which she said she had dropped a flatiron in the old days. And she remarked as well, from her prim and elastic mouth, that Robert's past had had its endearments. "For example, there was a whore in the town of Floyd named Betty," she whispered wryly. And whore as a word, tended to bring intermittent whines from the gathering, among them that cry of Grandmother DeWhit's which went "Robert DeWhit never had truck with a w-h-o-r-e."

"It's hardly a thing to be ashamed of," Dannie responded.

"Nor is the dead one's own parlor the place to bring it up," Grandmother said back.

They looked at each other icily.

Dannie said, "Robert was just an active person."

Grandmother DeWhit said, "I shall smack your mouth."

"Here, here," said Uncle Jericho Valeu DeWhit. "For example," he said, "the deceased once played upon the clarinet in Winnie Goings's corn field in his drawers. Likely as not Robert enjoyed it."

The red-mouthed, serpentine Aunt Toy Trilby Slide, *née* DeWhit, giggled from deep inside herself and sucked quickly on her own piece of popcorn. She said, "I mean we really ought to remember the good things, Ella Mae. For certainly Robert was never one to run from the light side."

"But it was the change which killed him," Cousin Dannie said, looking at Grandmother DeWhit contemptuously.

"And the climate."

"Worry with the mill and his chickens and the war."

"Remember the former years?"

"Remember when Robert got his foot caught."

"Was that, too, the year that Alexandria Cart accused him of *admiratio?*"

"Ha, ha, ha . . . ha, ha, ha!"

"Oh how he loved."

"And laughed."

"How he loved God's word as well."

"And the Thirty-eighth Chapter of Genesis!"

"Ha, ha, ha . . . ha, ha, ha!"

The air grew thick with such conduct. It was fashioned by the words themselves, and I found myself attending to memories of Grandfather and what had been similar events (though I had not perhaps known it), and there was an urge for me to add, "Once he called Great-aunt Beans Zip and Grandmother Zap."

I thought that I could have added even further judgments as well; I remembered the old face at church, the many times he had napped and waked up exactly in time to disagree with the Reverend over an issue he did not even hear. There were as well the fearsome times when he would use words that I could not understand; all the lost hours when you did not even know where he was. As all of his remarks to me were statements which I believed urgent and meaningful, so also his actions, which now got discussed in a way that I had never heard before, became a conveyance of a new feeling of attachment toward the old man. I saw myself, therefore, suddenly defending my grandfather. I remembered lying on his stomach and feeling there the impulses which only in recollection had caused me to reaffirm that he could not be dead. I wanted to stand once again and make my unpopular statement, but Mother, knowing it by instinct and tired of hearing it, kept on me, with her eyes, the same restraint that she kept on Grandmother DeWhit with her arms.

Cousin Dannie stood on the hearth before the fireplace and gripped the four-pronged poker as if it were a baton. And she waved it in the air, first down in a straight line, upward then in a 22½-degree angle, still upward in a convex arc, shortly, over to the right in the figure of a turn, and finally a last upward flourish. At the piano was Uncle Jericho, propped upon the music rack, while Aunt Toy Trilby Slide leaned at his left on the finial of an onyx ash stand.

Mother and Grandmother and Elizabeth and I sat alongside one another in front of them and next to the old man's presently vacant chair.

"I do recall," went on Cousin Dannie, "once taking the part of Cleopatra opposite Robert in the part of Antony."

"Tell us of it," sucked Uncle Jericho, his hand swished in a praying fold, his face immobile like a bust.

"I shall," she said, and "first," she said, "you must know that we had fashioned our own costumes. I wore the pettifrock of my intrepid Great-aunt Judalon. I wore many baubles in consequence of this exquisite pettifrock, you see. My hair I put up like this, as one would do were one to play Cleopatra accurately. And then, you see, Robert came on as Antony. He wore

Great-uncle Morris's cape as a pant, draped from his buttocks with a belt and tied upside down at the ankles with rope."

"I remember the performance," said Uncle Jericho. He and the other relations, you could see, were growing ever so interested in Grandmother DeWhit, who already was beginning to be annoyed. Mother held her tightly.

"Only," continued Cousin Dannie, "Robert had not been careful to close the front of the cape, and he had as well removed his underclothing to perform. The consequence was, of course, that I saw it."

"It indeed."

"How well did you see it?"

"Well enough. A most preposterously marvelous thing! He was not aware; hardly aware until he had come well into the first of his actions."

"Had he not anything to say?"

"It was Antony's first line as I recall, and then he knew."

"What did he do?"

"He smiled widely. He smiled widely at first."

Cousin Dannie smiled elfishly. She drew the poker in a quick jerk, and slowly let it down from there, in the air, to the thin leftovers of a log in the fireplace.

"There," she added, "he stood and smiled widely."

"Then, then?"

"Jericho, Jericho, must you *really* know?"

"I must know," said Aunt Toy.

"*I* must," said Grandmother DeWhit, no longer hiding

her full interest. She twisted her hands loose from Mother and stood to confront her tormentors. "You said this much and now you must say the rest," she said.

"I shall tell you on a condition," Dannie responded coyly, "and the condition, Ella Mae, is that you do what I ask."

It was not exactly a look which Grandmother then exchanged with the relations from Floyd. It was as though she had suddenly been caught in an expected trap. You could tell that she sensed even more than that. Her voice seemed eventually to break into a hum, and there was a grunt which suggested an even further apprisal. You only heard the relatives breathing in satisfied and detached titters. Aunt Toy Trilby Slide seemed intent on mocking the air itself, breathing in irregular, lapping pants as if to tease. You knew that they had planned it carefully.

"If you think" — Grandmother DeWhit quailed — "that I shall make a fool of myself merely to know whether or not my deceased loved one exposed himself to you, you are indeed a type of fiend and you have upset my frame of mind."

"But you *want* to know. Look at it this way — I know that you want to know because you have never, uh — seen . . ."

The ugly, swarthy woman cackled with the noise of a seam being ripped and Grandmother's face grew tortured.

Cousin Dannie went on, "Manifest your conscience now that he's dead, Ella. You must tell us how it was that you came to have Robert. Speak of the conception of your child, your child Emma Ruth. Tell us all how Robert *loved* you . . . and about this uh — bastard daughter of yours . . ."

Grandmother said frantically, "You are impertinent. All you will ever hear from me is that Robert and I loved."

In the room a wild music was on the air like voices crying for mercy, and you could not be quite sure what was going on. You heard all of them going at once, and Grandmother attempting to shush them. But you heard as well the apprisals which went up there into the rafters of the great parlor almost secretly.

"You loved indeed," Dannie cried. "You lured Robert, dear, because you could breed and he wanted a son. Now that Robert is dead, let us have the truth — you lured him in his infirmity, and you already had that bastard child."

"How vile you are," Grandmother screamed.

"But there was Robert," Dannie said, growing all the more determined. "There he was with the cape outspread while I played Cleopatra. He smiled widely and invited me. He asked if I did not want to look more closely. He said that since I had seen only partially, I might as well see the rest."

"The purpose of course was that you might be certain of his chastity?" asked Aunt Toy.

"No, rather that I might understand his manhood," replied Cousin Dannie. She crossed the room and stood exactly at the front of the fireplace, gouging at the nearly destroyed wood. "He was but fourteen at the time, and what I saw was primarily the *deformity* of it," she said. "It had no more than one child in it, I swear, no more than *one* and he told me so."

"Emma *is* that child," Grandmother cried.

"She is *not*," Cousin Dannie replied. "Robert even wept," she said, "and he said 'oh my one child must be a son, and I must find a woman who can breed.' He pleaded for me to understand and I did, but now he is dead and he never loved you, Ella Mae."

Mother coddled Grandmother DeWhit. She smoothed the weeping face with her handkerchief and Grandmother could barely speak. She only kept saying that Dannie was wrong and evil.

"In the name of God, leave," she cried and she said over and over again, "Robert and I loved, we loved." Then she whispered in deep sorrow to all of them, "Why?"

Uncle Jericho laughed aloud. He said that the De-Whits of the town of Floyd expected either an "inheritance" or a public acknowledgment. He said that they were tired of the masquerade.

He put his hand high in the air to suggest that he had said the final say. Then the gathering was silent and you did not know what was going on again. Perhaps I recall a little remorse even from the relations, but they did say that they were going to bring off a lawsuit. Elizabeth told me quickly that I was too young to understand that.

Mother's own tears were an embarrassed sort, and

I mean that I thought I saw her looking in the futile way which she used for Daddy Egan. She held me tightly.

When the relations had left without being asked, Grandmother and Mother embraced each other and Grandmother emerged completely in tears. In the nearly cold room, the old worn-out fire log was the suitable token of the helplessness which seemed to prevail. I was aloft the dark ottoman of my mother's chair, watching her with forbearance. It seemed that I was supposed to comfort her in a way, and so I put myself into her lap and kissed her face.

I said, "I see that Grandfather is supposed to be dead, but he is not really."

Mother smiled at that but slightly, and then we were all aware of the most important part of the aftereffects of that so-called funeral: that Daddy Egan now stood there in the foyer looking quite unhappy again. He had let himself in from the back of the house, apparently to avoid being involved in the quarrel.

He said, "I am just so sorry, Emma; sorry about all of it."

Mother tried not to weep and she only embraced him faintly while Grandmother DeWhit stood by. I, on the other hand, crossed the room in a flash. I shook his hand ecstatically and put my head in his stomach.

* 14 *

WHATEVER THE REVELATIONS, the inheritances, they were secondary to that look which was on Grandmother's face. Like a mortician, she eyed Father with dissective instincts while he told her how sorry he was that Grandfather had died. She grumbled even then that he had not said it adequately and Father threw up his hands.

Grandmother left hastily, and crying. And she ordered Elizabeth and me to bed.

I could not sleep. I did not want to sleep, first of all, but I *could* not because I worried that he would get away without my seeing him. I went secretly looking for Father, then, gliding the staircase without being seen and finally able to get into the closet where the view was superb, where in fact I was able to be sure if *she* left. And I would know where *he* was too.

They talked for a moment and Father said, "Well she is going to have to come off her high horse one of these days, meantime she's mucked *us* up!"

"Now Egan," Mother said soporifically. Characteristically, she carried a set of new bed linens and some red towels which she offered him for the guest room. "Mama gave him a good house. Father is dead."

"And better off, poor man!"

"You just don't know Mama, and you just don't know about being a first family and running a house like this. First, it takes its toll and then it's hard. Besides, I am the one who gave Mother her disposition. I am the one who discovered that principle noblesse oblige."

Father answered, "I hate your goddamn mother and I hate this goddamn house!"

He wobbled slightly and then you knew that he was drunk and Mother said, "Egan, you're drunk and I don't want you in the house if you're drunk and you *know* what I think of drunkenness."

"You-know-what-I-think-of-drunkenness," he mocked with a falsetto tone. He stood taller, tall as possible, and commenced to take off his clothes.

He said, "Emma, you know that there is a war with Hitler, and now I have to go over there. I have to fight in Poland. I might as well."

Father took his liquor bottle out of his coat and his nonchalance seemed altogether contradictory to the fear that was in his eyes. Mother gasped aloud and she almost cried but she held on to her towels. She looked around the room as he did too, though both of them searched for words.

"Now I'm going to have you before I go off to god-damn Poland," he said.

Despite her astonishment with the announcement, Mother was hurrying to the doorway, and she prepared to replace the linens in the closet. She was then crying and she was fiddling with the top face cloth and folding it. Father concluded his undressing and there he was naked with his enormous body flexed out and agitated in the glassy light. He took several wild gulps of the liquor and let it run down his chin and off like a falls onto his chest. I could see that it ran through the hair where he rubbed it in. He opened his legs and let the liquor drain there too, and you could see that it was as enormous as the rest of him.

"I'm tired," he said, "and I want you to come here."

"No."

"You didn't even teach the children my name. Daddy Egan," he mocked again, "as if old man DeWhit was just as much a father."

"I have your clean linens here," Mother said.

Father went toward her quickly from the sofa, and it was sticking out as if it were on a leash and he was towering over her busily. He was a sticky brown, blinking his eyes to get his footing while the sinews of his body constricted visibly.

"Egan dear," she said, "now Egan dear."

He said, "You heard me!"

Then all along Mother clung to the towels between them, and she fought. Her free hand pulled out for a rope in the air and the fingers stretched like scissors into an invisible cloth. Solemnly she cried, "Oh it's rotten, that war, oh it's a terrible feeling, oh Egan, years, acts, intimidations. I can't do *it*."

"The hell you can't," he said.

He opened her housedress and separated the breasts in his hands, thickly cupped one into his mouth which, like a ferrule, drew the flesh into a tight purse.

She said, "Oh my God, oh my God," and Father grunted but gently and they were on the sofa while their shadows fell upon the ceiling with all the Ionic columns of the furniture.

"Now don't you think it was rather a silly thing for you to *enlist?*"

"What the hell else was there?"

"Sh —."

"I hate this goddamn house . . ."

"Egan."

"And besides, it's duty; they're all going; they're all on their way to Poland these days."

"Poland, Poland . . ."

"Poland, Pole, ha, ha, po ha, ha . . ."

"Egan, now, Egan, this isn't right, this, this isn't . . . Egan."

"*Pol*and, *Pol*and, *Pol*and . . . !"

There was a longing and instinctive feeling, even then, which told me about them. It was a threadlike substance going in my flesh which was like the sensations on the balustrade. And Mother was touching him in the same way she often touched me when she came out on the porch before supper at night; when she would stand in front of me and bury my face in her stomach. Besides, it was as Tolly Butterworth had suggested, though at last it was also a matter of sound; liquid noises which I associated with the movements. He had her down like that and quiet and she smiled amidst the kisses and the housedress fell open on the edge of the sofa. And off. And down onto the floor. Her hair was down and Father removed the towels. There was a sound of moisture again, and then it was all a sort of light too.

"I wanted you," Mother said. "Mama is so helpless and she brought me out of that terrible Mill Hill where I was born. You know that I don't even know who my father is, and there is the truth of the matter. I have to be grateful."

"Don't talk about that."

"But, Egan, you must understand."

"Will you go with me? When I get back from Poland, will you go with me?"

". . . yes, Egan."

Mother's hair was wet and shimmering; flowed down the pillow and rested at the top of her breasts. The differences between Father and her were only the faint tones of color on their faces.

Father said, "Well, if only there was time."

He told her that he must leave in the early morning and he told her that he must go and kiss the children good night. Many times he repeated how rotten it was — how rotten now that he had her — that the war . . . Then Mother had gone to sleep under him. He rose and looked at her and touched her. At last he lifted her and carried her away upstairs.

I got up from my place and went to the parlor sofa where I sat and put my hands on the pillows and tried to figure it out. Father's smell was still there and Mother's, but it was his which had that feeling of great power. Then Father was returning abruptly and was saying, "When did *you* come in here?"

I said, "I saw you and Mother doing love from the closet and don't tell me that that was not what you were doing, sir. Now Mother does not have any more problem with her bottom parts — does she — as they say. You have fixed it."

Daddy Egan looked back in the direction of the closet and then he looked at the sofa. He did not say anything at first but he laughed. It was not a drunken laugh by any means and then he got a dust cloth which he used to mop up the spilled liquor on the coffee table. Still naked, he scratched himself *there* and took the cloth to it.

He said, "Well, I don't say I didn't, and if you saw, you saw."

If I recall correctly, he had got to sitting again and

smoking a cigarette and that was the moment when he motioned me close to him. I went to his lap and held on to him more tightly than I had held to Grandfather. He was not fleshy and the hair was not wiry.

My head was on his stomach. He touched it firmly while he talked about that business of having to go off to Poland. He ran his hands from the back of my head onto his own chest and whispered quietly, at last, and in a kind of reminiscence.

"Yes, it was doing love that you saw."

I said, "I have learned it all now. There is a riddle for it, isn't there? And there is Tolly Butterworth who knows those special words, and there is Grandfather, who knows even more than Tolly and isn't really dead."

The remarks openly puzzled Father. He did not reply to me; he only drew me closer. At last he breathed on me specially and whispered, "Meantime, if you ever want to do *it* (ha, ha) be sure you wash off and pee good. There will come a time, and then you will know," he said.

"Very well, sir," I said.

He said, "I'll write to you from Poland where I am going for this war. I will tell you a few other things and then I will be back."

"Where is Poland, sir?"

Daddy Egan by then had thought just a little with the apparent contentment which he felt, and then he had gone off to sleep.

❋ 15 ❋

You must accept that both the DeWhit women only gave distinguished grimaces when, in the morning, they found me like that on Father's stomach and him naked and the air thick with the remains of his drunk. It was only that each of them was particularly disoriented because they threw up their hands and you would have thought for the moment that Mother had forgotten her decisions of the night before. Nor had Grandmother been anything but aghast when she said, "Get him out of here and get him away before I worry myself sick. First Robert dies and now this." All you saw after that was Father's distressed eyes pleading with Mother to come with him to the door while swiftly he dressed himself and kissed Elizabeth and me. At the last minute, as well, he propped up his shoulders from within, and was suddenly resigned. Finally he went to the kitchen where Grandmother had started to slam the refrigerator door. You heard the door slamming and not slamming, and at last a screech which brought Grandmother back to the parlor sighing, "Oh Emma, oh Emma, he called me Zip; he *touched* me just like a man!"

In the room Mother had put herself near the foyer door, her face drawn far down and somehow cold, though she wrung her hands in characteristic fashion and breathed so that you could hear it. Emergent in her eyes, the thin scale of futility showed while Father paused in the foyer and looked back to her. She nodded, but only that.

When he had gone off on the Vermen road and when the house was also quiet with that sort of an air which suggests that nothing is true, Mother smiled only a little and pulled me harshly to herself on the sofa. I was thinking how quiet she seemed underneath the movement, almost as if she might have been acting out a part. I was uncertain of everything, to be sure; I did not know, for instance, what it meant that she stared at me a long time before speaking, and that, when she finally did speak, her words settled into a tone of faint distrust.

"What did you do?" she demanded. "How did you get down here like that? What are you doing here in your pajamas still and what did your father tell you?"

"I saw you and him doing love. He said that he is going to a place called Poland, but he said that he will be back."

"Your father is silly and childish sometimes," she

said. Mother changed her look to a quizzical one. And that made her seem unwilling to hear herself. She gazed around the room and she blew out her breath in long heavy sighs, which were substitutes for speaking.

"At least you don't have any more problems with your bottom parts," I said.

"My God in heaven, child, my God in heaven!"

And her hands went to my face as if she were going to hit me. She mumbled inaudibly and said yes to something, frowning and kissing me, at last, so that I did not like it. With that, she was also saying a poem, though it was only the rhyme of it that I heard. She looked at her hands and at my face, especially at the skin, and for the moment seemed to be testing its softness. Then she whispered that there ought to be words for what she wanted to say. Also, she said, "I am not sure of what I have done; there are just better things, there must be."

I was thinking that I must comfort my mother, and I was thinking that perhaps I might help her figure out whatever it was that bothered her. As I felt considerably more adult on account of the evening with Father, I also had in mind to tell her that she should not worry herself.

But presently in came Grandmother DeWhit, running down from the sun porch.

"Oh, Emma, they're here again. I can see the DeWhits from Floyd coming up the driveway in a Chevrolet. I know what they want."

Pumped like a new bicycle tire, and hastily shaping her chignon to the left, Mother approached the curtains to look while the relations, not bothering themselves to knock, poked their way in. It was all the former positions reproduced and you had, to be sure, Cousin Dannie presiding at the poker. Her voice up high before we had ever got seated, she emphasized that they had come for a showdown; but leaning there, Grandmother asserted that she planned no more revelations of conscience to speak of. Calmly she said it, and with an element of laughter.

"Don't be trying to laugh this off, Ella Mae DeWhit. Don't try to laugh us off in this house full of bastards. Personally it is not funny."

Grandmother, on the sofa by that time, was next to Mother and she was pretending to be more amused when the visitors did their preliminaries which first of all deplored her choice of a tombstone. And they deplored as well the epitaph which went *Robert DeWhit Who Made Allowances*. Aunt Toy Trilby Slide opted for a sarcophagus, but Uncle Jericho believed more in mausoleums.

Entirely resolute, Grandmother DeWhit turned her head from them; she had learned from the Reverend Brendelle to talk to the fireplace as if she were Moses, and in that view she said, "I won't change any of it. He was my husband. I loved him. I served him. He left his money to us."

"To that child."

"To that silly child."

You were mostly aware of the rhythm in that, and that it tightened Grandmother's courage immeasurably. Her voice began to trail lightly to a new condescension as she told how legal it all was and how they would have a h-e-l-l of a time changing anything.

"That is not the point," said Cousin Dannie in a masculine way.

There were certain mad laughs of satisfaction too.

"Money in the hands of a child."

"But *we* don't care about that especially."

"What we care about is the perfidy."

"And your deception, Ella Mae."

Only as if she needed to, Grandmother got up on her toes with indignation and not spitefully. She said, "Stop it!" and her body shook and she held to Mother, pleading and humbly asking them to leave her alone. She finally wept profusely and gave that speech which told how hard she had worked and how she had been forced in 1917 to be violated. She said she could not help it and then she said 1929 was a bad year too. She braced herself.

But as that was done and you could tell it, you also saw that her eyes were coming up brightly at last; and they were quite sober with what instantly proved to be an inspiration. Grandmother looked at me specially and pointed and said, "Just the same, Robert has got a heir" (she said it pronouncing the h, in her fashion), and stepped to my side and pulled me up.

"A heir, a heir," she sang, "and you can tell what you please."

Now the early August day had somehow caught the chill of a foreshadowed autumn. Somehow caught the certainty of her cold idea while, for the moment, she also went to scratching her head and pacing. They said how silly she was, but she said that she would concede nothing but an additional angel on the tombstone. And the point is that she did not budge.

The point is that she had acted that way and the DeWhits of Floyd left in bitter anger.

She followed them to the door triumphantly as well, the distant tears forming up and her relevant posture finely transposed into a measure of pride. Yet she moaned and wept and sometimes blew her breath.

Then in the jaundiced hallway, hastily, she rang up a certain engraver whom she engaged to add her version of Grandfather's epitaph to all the DeWhit possessions, memorial or otherwise. That full measure of her frivolity, her honesty, maybe even her true pleasure, showed well in this litany:

DEWHIT MEMORIAL CHURCH
THROUGH THE GENEROSITY OF ROBERT S. DEWHIT
WHO MADE ALLOWANCES

ROBERT S. DEWHIT MEMORIAL BRIDGE
IN CONJUNCTION WITH THE GOVERNMENTS OF THE USA
AND THE CITY OF KORNELIUS ABOVE THE SOUTH SHOALS
AND ROBERT S. DEWHIT
WHO MADE ALLOWANCES

ROBERT S. DEWHIT BUBBLER FOUNTAIN
2 JULY MDCCCCXXV UPON THE OCCASION OF THE
ROBERT S. DEWHIT MEMORIAL PARK AND SHUFFLE BOARD
WHO MADE ALLOWANCES

THE ROBERT S. DEWHIT MEMORIAL PARK AND SHUFFLE BOARD
PRESENTED TO THE CITY OF KORNELIUS ABOVE THE SHOALS
BY ROBERT S. DEWHIT
WHO MADE ALLOWANCES

(all of it guarded and preserved in the name of
God by Ella Mae DeWhit, grandmother to the
heir of Mr. Robert S. DeWhit who loved her
without doubt)

She had got to be happier with that, but for the
moment she had been entirely put off by my presence.
I had tried to comfort her too, but she pushed me away
immediately. She had got to winding the clocks very
well without me, and her hand went up like a broken
lever to wipe away the sweat.

At the bottom of the staircase, fully in the morning
light which freshly lit the dust motes in their first movements about the foyer, I had considered that maybe old
Grandfather might not have approved of my attitude.
I thought of words which he might have used toward
her while in the air the old ashen face of the prophet
flashed on and off like a torch. I was not startled and the
bright sun helped me to sustain him there as I thought
of what it must be to have all those things which I
was now supposed to have.

"It is about time that you came back," I said, though

from time to time the face paled as Father's did on the balustrade. Then Grandfather was there quite vividly.

Mother had not come in and neither had Elizabeth. They were all in the kitchen buzzing on the subject of the relations from Floyd and whether they would be back. I went to the closet, therefore, and smelled the Kirby vacuum snout for the pleasure of it. Grandfather followed me, it seemed, and the first of his enchantments had to do with the way he seemed to change back and forth into Daddy Egan. I did not have on Father's drawers, but I took them down, out of the baseball uniform, and held them. I remembered the touch of Father's belly, the mass of warm and hard flesh. The touch of the hair had also but recalled Grandmother's statement of my inheritance and then I thought I knew what she meant. I said to the old man, "I know why I am your hair." And I said, "I am your hair as Grandmother has said; and if I am your hair, I am better Father's hair. I slept on both your bellies, but *longer* on his."

"Go with your father," the ghost said, smiling and huffing a clean grunt from his old caved-in chest.

✳ 16 ✳

IT WAS A MATTER OF WAITING for mail deliveries; a matter of many things that Father was not there again. That he was in Poland, which they explained only as "faraway," and somehow farther even than Richmond, was also that he could not tell me the truth about either my mother's or my grandmother's behavior. And all the while the latter moaned, the former practiced the piano and rubbed her face in Jergen's lotion. She did finally insist, however, that it was time for me to start becoming a serious poet as it was both near-time for me to start school and near-time for me to be having thoughts about the theory of noblesse oblige. For that, Mother's sessions with new words became the likely substitute for the Bible readings which were no longer even spoken of; her premises being, first, that I ought to know how to spell if I was ever going to know how to write, and, second, that words like *foolishness* and *non-*

sense, which were my choices, hardly seemed the fitting ones to put into a poem.

All the while, for instance, when she was teaching me how to spell *do, wish,* and *seem,* she was as well about the business of looking out strangely into the air and there quickly throwing back her hair to listen and then to shrug.

I knew that *she* was listening for the mail too.

Ultimately my mother got to allowing me to use words which I had secretly taken from her own scrapbook, but she did not realize where I had got them. For the pride of it she had almost daily said, "How long your grandmother and I have planned that the household should have its beauties!" Which was first a sort of motto and then the very words which at last formed the hardest of my spelling tasks:

to plan   the household   should have   beauties

But she always stared pensively around the room when she said it, almost as if she ought to subject the principle to the approval of the air itself. And she would be momentarily discomfited and rub her hand on her chin. From there Mother often fingered certain objects in the room, and finally put her fingers wildly on the piano keys where she played six measures of the "Black Hawk Waltz" and said that it was one of the *finer things*. One of the finer things, she said, which we DeWhits had and other people did not; as it was also, she went on, the very reason why we were the first family and why, indeed, I must be a poet. Why I must learn my lessons; why I must bear myself well; why I must ignore the relations from Floyd; why I must not be careless in trusting my father's deceptions; why I must stay away from Tolly Butterworth.

As for the last two, she never wished to answer me when I said, "Then why did you get down there like that without your clothes?"

Instead, Mother took from her alligator purse a red-covered little book with a rose on it and said, "Here is a scrapbook for you to collect what you have to say in. You must put in any word which I approve and none of those which I do not. For now I will write them for you, but one day you will learn how to do this yourself."

Mother told me that it was a matter of finding the right words for what was beautiful and what was good, she said, and she said it was all very much like Shakespeare when he proposed:

> what silent love hath writ
> belongs to love's fine wit.

"Well of course I understand *that*," I pretended, and so I tried to tell her, first, that old Grandfather had spoken similarly. I told her that he had said how beautiful she was, though finally I told her that the important thing about Grandfather was that he made me think of Father who brought to mind this my first poem:

> the world within
> my father's skin
> is like all men

"My God in heaven, there you go again with those references to your father's body and to strange and peculiar means of speech."

"Is that *not* a poem," I asked. "You have *within, skin, men.*" I traced a hook to my lips and rubbed them. Then I clicked my teeth with what I thought was a better poem, my second poem:

> Father's name
> is just the same
> as my name

"Better . . . but . . ."

She wrote it in the scrapbook reluctantly. Holding the book forward, she also showed me how she had done it and it looked as I had thought it should. She rubbed her hands on the words and smiled at me. Mother's face saddened slowly.

I also said, "Don't you miss him?"

And then Mother pursed her lips as the movement of her face came back. She, at that, had got determined to ignore my question, but you could see that she was thinking about it in her own way. She asked me if I had other lines in return, however, other lines, perhaps, about matters which did not have to do with Father.

> The moon and pines
> Play games in whines

"Oh, yes, very good."

Doing love
is
being above.

"Egan, child, enough of that I said!"

But at last came the thing which Mother had waited for in the air, and it was the sound, out front, of the dray truck which never came on Wednesdays unless Blaze Burnett was out there to deliver the mail. You knew it was the mail as Mother's face was sustained in an upward but solicitous lilt which she denied by moving slowly.

Elizabeth came in all flippantly discussing the war and saying that Adolf Hitler looked a certain way. She put her teeth like a horse and brushed them a little and then she, as well, said that this letter now arriving would doubtless prove that Father was doing well against Hitler's horse calvary.

"Calvary, calvary," she said.

And Mother, acting vexed outright, even delayed the opening of the letter to criticize my sister's words. What you had was Grandmother DeWhit coming there too, frightened and solicitous but in a different way. You had her first trying to take the letter from Mother, and then telling her not to read it because it was likely a plea for her to come and do *it* in Poland too.

Mother neither laughed nor grew upset at that, but she stared at both Grandmother DeWhit and Elizabeth with evident bewilderment. She held their hands, in fact, and shook her head a little.

Finally Mother read the letter out loud and she read it in a decidedly absent-minded way:

Dear Emma and all. You see that I am here doing my duty now. It has been awhile, and how are you? I am fine, and I am going to come home as soon as possible and I am sorry that we only just had started to get together. But I will be back there and we can go then and live in the house which I have built for you in Vermen. At this moment Mama and Wexie are taking care of it, but not for long. I will come get you and take you there. I do love you all, and tell the boy this.

I will be back soon.

Love and yours, Egan.

Grandmother DeWhit fled the room sobbing and Mother raised her head seeming unaware that she had read the letter as she did. She scanned Elizabeth's face and mine, and she was suddenly occupied with my sister's smile.

Elizabeth said, "I told you that Father must be doing well in Poland against Hitler's calvary."

Mother said, "Oh oh dear, Elizabeth, the word is *cavalry!*"

She let the letter fall to the floor as she grimaced further at a puzzled Elizabeth, though finally she was also whimpering in another futile manner, clasping her hands together and calling out Father's name.

"Oh," she said, "oh, will it ever work out, Egan? Years, act, intimidations: what will we ever do with that child?"

Mother paced for the moment and she forgot the letter. She started to talk to herself, then she laughed. She rose abruptly and listened to the air. She pulled me along with her to the parlor which was dark because Grandmother DeWhit had drawn the curtains. In there you heard the older woman sobbing beside the cloth armory. She was saying, "Oh, oh no," and she was biting on the edges of her fingers. "Whatever will I do, whatever?" She said pointblank that she had heard Mother read the letter. She had heard it all, and so now she *knew* that Mother's plan was to go off and leave her.

"I only suspected, but now I *know!*"

In the darkened parlor, in the middle of the floor, Grandmother commenced to whine in a new high tone, running her words together and moving her body like a dying wasp.

"It-is-only-just-for-*it*,   which-you-don't-need-Emma, only-just-so-that-he-can-have, and, Emma, well-so-that: isn't-it-enough-that-he-has-mistreated-you-under-the-pine-tree! And now you even feel a need for *it!* I never-had-that-need, and-thank-God-that . . ."

Grandmother went to the cloth armory then and took out the Sacred Bolts. She spread them on the floor and spread her hands in sweeping circles and rubbed them out in front of her. She might have once flinched briefly, but thereafter her eyes were cold and distant. She lay on the cloth and commenced to touch each section of it as though it were holy. She called Grandfather's name and Mother's, and she kept whining, "Oh, oh dear, oh dear."

Mother put her fingers to her head in terror, though her breath issued slowly and diplomatically.

"No-no," she said, but she began to groan as well, and you saw that she got down there, too, on the cloth, and started to pick at a flaw in the design just like Grandmother. I pulled at her sleeve and asked her to get up. But Mother would not listen to me, and so I took the letter which still lay on the floor and went with it to the closet where I pretended to have understood how far away Father was.

✳ 17 ✳

AND THERE WAS THE MATTER of the letter, and the matter of Grandmother, and the matter, at last, of the coming of autumn which, under the circumstances, might have been as brown and as futile as coffee ground through a fourth brewing. As for the letter, I kept it well hidden and pondered it in the linen closet, though Grandmother was often prone to be looking for it so that she could burn it. And Grandmother was also prone to run off to the cemetery, where she would sit beneath the arms of one of Grandfather's tombstone angels and say, "Let-me-tell-you-about-*it!*"

Mother had to be occupied, therefore, with keeping her indoors. Which made the time darker. Which, in fact, kept us all out of touch, though Mother did have two devices for holding down the queen of the house-hold: often she took her the Sacred Bolts and helped her turn them; on Saturdays she regularly took her off to the Sheba Beauty Parlor where both of them got a Facial and a Blue Rinse.

The result was that Elizabeth and I were left alone with this advice: Stay away from Tolly Butterworth and the Nigger Ruth girls.

I was anxious for school to begin because Mother had no time much to help me with new words. And my sister openly admitted that she would go to school mainly to be with her Clyde; and mainly, she said, because she could also feel certain stirrings in her bottom parts.

That second Saturday, when Mother had bundled Grandmother DeWhit up and taken her down to the beauty parlor, I was in my closet lying on my back smelling the linens which were in heaps and clusters and organized according to starchiness by Nigger Ruth. I was looking at Father's letter and I was talking to Grandfather DeWhit about it. The door was ajar and you heard Elizabeth and Clyde sneaking around out there in a whisper without bothering with the lights. She had brought him in the back door and she had said, "I just had to see you, and it has been so long a time."

"Well everybody knows what the trouble is," he sighed. "The DeWhits of Floyd have told it around."

"Let's not talk of fatuitous things," Elizabeth said. She touched him on the shoulder and I scrambled to my knees so as to hide behind the vacuum cleaner and not be seen. Elizabeth looked for me, but she did not find me. Then she said, "We have to be careful." She touched him on his belly and Clyde laughed aloud. He was looking into the great parlor mirror and smoothing out the folds in the back of his trousers which stuck between the cheeks of his buttocks. Once he picked at his enormous groin, which Elizabeth watched intently.

"We have to be careful," Elizabeth muttered. "You know what Mother would say. You know what Grandmother would *do*."

Elizabeth lifted the largest of the down-filled pillows from the sofa and held it in front of her. Embracing it, she rubbed her chin against the top edge.

"We've never talked so well before," she continued. "And so what should we talk about, dearest Clyde?"

"Don't call me dearest," Clyde said.

He shaped out his bulge so that it distracted Elizabeth again. He stood sideways, which accentuated the pelvic bulge further.

"Tell me why you aren't afraid to be in this house," Elizabeth teased.

He replied, "I'm just not."

"Dearest Clyde," Elizabeth said, "can't I come over there and put my arms around you and can't I touch you?"

Clyde answered her, "Don't call me dearest," and went over there before her instead and fingered her beads, twisting them and putting his long arms out against the doorjamb behind my sister. His voice had got about it a steady moan, but it was not as if he had wanted it to be that way. Leaning against her with his whole body, Clyde put his arms on Elizabeth's waist. He removed the pillow.

"D'ya feel me?"

Elizabeth said nothing. Her face lowered onto Clyde's shoulder. Her eyes closed of a sudden. Elizabeth writhed while he began to remove her clothes. He did it step by step as he was shrugging his shoulders and looking at everything.

"I know how to do this. You just be still. It's real love."

He stood in front of her exactly so that I could also see a small vertical side of her body when he moved to the right or to the left in the fast and steady glide.

"You see how it is?" he said.

At length Clyde stood quietly and limply away from Elizabeth and so you could see her as he apparently wanted to. She looked up toward him and she went on leaning against the wall. She was looking at Clyde as he buttoned his trousers and her face pleaded and she held her hands then in front of her, pulling up her petticoat from the floor. The undergarment enticed Clyde further, and he bent down to remove it.

"You didn't undress. You took *my* clothes, but you didn't undress at all."

"The man ain't supposed to. I was already ready."

"I want to see!"

Elizabeth leaned once more against the wall and let

go the petticoat. Clyde stared fiercely. He grabbed
her tightly and they fell together before the wall. They
let themselves onto the floor, too, where my sister started
to unbutton Clyde's shirt. She touched his face with her
fingertips. Ripping at his shirt front, she was working
on his belt also. Then, as Elizabeth's hand dipped hun-
grily into the top of Clyde's unbuttoned trousers and
into the elastic of his drawers, she gasped. Clyde lay
entranced with his own smile, but she knelt above him,
pulling further at the top of his drawers until you could
see it. In her hands Elizabeth drew out a massive tuft
of absorbent cotton big as a cantaloupe and big enough
to have explained everything. The instrument itself was
small and pimply, and Elizabeth laughed out loud.

Clyde got up from there half dazed and he was
carelessly letting his trousers drop to his ankles.

"So I padded it," he said.

"It's funny."

Elizabeth pushed herself toward him again and
mewed how it all meant that they were certainly in love
for sure. She picked up her clothes piece by piece
while Clyde puzzled clumsily. He tried following her
and he said that they must get married and she said
yes. Elizabeth buzzed at him with her lips pooched out
and went to the sofa still naked.

"Perhaps we could run off to the marrying town
of Huanebango," she said.

"It's decided," Clyde replied, scratching his arse and
confused. "Don't you want to finish what we were
doing?"

"I just want to sit here without my clothes. First we'll have to tell Mother . . . or maybe we shouldn't; maybe we should just go off, like that and then . . ."

Clyde, visibly exasperated, was snatching up his trousers and stumbling toward the foyer where he also attempted to rescue his cotton ball; and it was at this time very near my closet. Then he saw me in the closet.

He said, "Oh my dear Jesus God in heaven mercy!"

He pulled me out of the closet and flew me toward Elizabeth, who commenced to whine like a bending saw. I did not say anything at all, but she leaned against the wall. Clyde was fuming and clutching his cotton ball helplessly.

With the noise, Mother came in with her new chignon; Grandmother DeWhit came in with the crisp upsweep. The two of them were stone-faced and irate.

Elizabeth froze and Clyde pulled on his trousers in terror; and the game was of war and had the rubrics of a sideshow: Grandmother snatching up her kitchen broom and chasing Clyde as if he were a roach looking for the dark; he dodging the broom until at last he was at the door and could run: fleeing down the hill calling back to Elizabeth of their former plans. Elizabeth begged after him while Grandmother pursued frantically.

"Get that child while I get that one. Get the girl a douche," she yelled. "Get the syringe and get her to the toilet this instant for a douche. She's been to bed with Robert's child. A criminal act, Emma-get-the-poor-child-a-douche-as-she-has-done-it-and-it-is . . ."

She went off like that through the front door and was out there with the broom, off in the direction of the Mill Hill also, while Mother lifted Elizabeth's head peacefully to kiss her over and over again. For the moment her strange smile had returned from earlier days. But all you could hear was Grandmother DeWhit still screaming outside, her voice taut by then, up in the highest whining area, and she was crying, "Oh Emma, oh dear, what will this do to the family? The disgrace, the disgrace! The family is beset by even fouler things than the enemy within."

And then it was a matter of Mother's having stood before Elizabeth charitably with a syringe. Her eyes were the liquid consistency of ginger syrup, petitioning for interpretation as if there were no correct words for what she had wanted to say. This time her tears spilled off her face in a kinder sympathy, being in a way, genuine, as Elizabeth put herself calmly on the sofa in her pettifrock.

"You're not going to do that to me," she scoffed, whipping herself up from time to time and looking out the window behind her where you could see Grandmother DeWhit flying about the front yard to stalk a long-departed Clyde.

"I am no slave to enervating sleep," Elizabeth continued.

Mother said, "This is no time to quote the prophets, dear," and she added, "you know what will happen to you if you don't get this done."

She touched Elizabeth's forehead, brushing the hair which framed my sister in a soft white, the paleness of her body jailed by the stripes of the patterned sofa.

"I know what it means," Elizabeth said, "and I don't want to be washed out. I *love* him." Then she rose, breathing deeply, and gathered her clothing. She flung her dress across her shoulder and waded into her shoes. She walked triumphantly toward the foyer stairs. Finally she hardly seemed aware of Mother anymore, and neither was she aware that Grandmother suddenly had returned. She ignored the quiet whispers that accompanied her up the stairs. The rapt faces that saddled along in the rear spoke in terrified frowns, and nodded in some kind of reluctant affirmation and the women seized Elizabeth by both arms and carried her screaming to Mother's upstairs bathroom.

There Mother put Elizabeth on her lap upside down and poked in the syringe. Elizabeth's feet went in the air and she cried. Grandmother held the hot water bottle and she held it high, examining everything that was going on as if she were looking for special signs. She grunted momentarily and they picked Elizabeth up and put her on the toilet.

"Do it!"

Mother only looked soberly and her former sadness was not gone. She was forced to put the syringe down so that she could wipe the tears away, and when you finally heard the sound of the water going where it was supposed to, she sniffed in a great relief that annoyed

Grandmother DeWhit. What you had then was this tableau of Grandmother with the used hot water bottle, Mother was sitting on the side of the bathtub, and Elizabeth, asquat the toilet, was folding her hands like a martyr.

I was waiting until Mother had tried to comfort her and Grandmother had left.

Frightened, I was thinking that it must somehow have been my fault.

When Elizabeth got up and waddled forward, she swelled up her shoulders in her fashion model's way and she looked lovely. While Mother wept and ran fearfully to her downstairs bedroom, I stood beside Elizabeth and put my arms around her as she started down the stairs and commenced to put on her clothes.

"I really am going off from here," she said. "The both of them are horrible. They both are crazy."

I said hastily, "I am sorry, Elizabeth. There you were doing love, as I know, and it was all fine as Father has said, but, Elizabeth, what was I to do?"

My sister embraced me without being vindictive. She was very adult, it seemed, and she carved with her eyes a singular inverted V down into my face.

I said, "Are you different now?"

"No," she said, "but I am going to face this issue. They really are crazy and I will go away with my Clyde. There is this famous marrying town of Huanebango where I will go. I am uproared. South of here they marry at eleven. I am almost fifteen — don't you think I could pass for fifteen — and they don't ask questions south of here in that marrying town."

Elizabeth made herself up to be exuberant, which made her look like a goldfish coming up for food, and she continued to look upward where she seemed to be gathering special ideas.

She said, "First I can go down there to see Nigger Ruth and get some help from her girls. Clyde and I will go and then I will fetch up a business position as I am old for my age. Or perhaps I shall just become a fashion model for *Harper's Brassiere*."

"Good, Elizabeth."

"And I have decided it. I have decided it, and my evidence is that they washed me out with cold creme. Is it not enough to convince you?"

"I have never been washed out with cold creme," I said.

I put my face on my sister's shoulder. She warned me not to tell her plans to anybody and for the next few days she went to the fish pond regularly to think on her decision and sometimes she went to the farthest climb of Grandfather's hill where Clyde would be waiting.

Meantime, however, my sister was coming down with a severe case of the prickly heat which she blamed on the douche and which made her walk like Bathsheba on the way to be stoned. This delayed her plans for the moment though she had commenced already to avoid Mother and Grandmother DeWhit. Mother tried often to embrace Elizabeth. But it was Grandmother DeWhit who made the last straw by coming, the nearest Friday, and accosting Elizabeth with that word "w-h-o-r-e!"

Elizabeth had, despite her prickly heat, got her little white ladies' case and her red dress, which she put on Integer Vita, and started down the driveway. And the day was bleak with those sounds which came up from the river and suggested that it was receding and that the river was finally going to be smaller. The lesson was of many cuts and terrible impulses in the air and I felt it as if I had suddenly been propped up and bombarded with demands to be older.

Elizabeth said, "Well, I am definitely going now, and you must tell Father about it. I know that Mother has not heard from him again, and I know that he had those plans for us. I must go, however. One must do what one must do."

Elizabeth stumbled her way forward, conspicuously straddling her prickly heat. She spit in the driveway and locked up her belt, and each step became more determined. She lifted her wrist to her nose and drained the mucous.

"Goodbye and good luck," she said.

"I won't tell," I said.

"Oh tell them; they cannot find me. Nigger Ruth will help. I have left them a note on the piano and they will find out soon. But I will be gone. Do not tell them until I am gone. Goodbye and good luck."

Elizabeth looked at me for a long time silently. She stopped her movements for a moment, aware of my fear. Her round face got sad but she became studied and elegant.

"Down there," she said, pointing toward the front yard, "is a certain pine tree. It is *the* pine tree, the one distant from the fish pond, the pretty one. And it is the one where Mother used to sit and comb her hair and read "Sonnets to the Pickinese." Father was here then, but you don't remember that. I thought you would like to know."

I ran along beside her. Elizabeth seemed to grow taller and then she was at the Vermen road which she crossed hastily. Across the way she was descending toward the Brush Pile and toward Nigger Ruth's house. I was shouting to her over the Chevrolets which went by. I was saying, "Goodbye, Elizabeth," and my sister kept on stumbling with her rash without looking back. At last she disappeared and I sat on the climb of Grandfather's hill. The air was thick in that way which I had remembered on Father's return. It was chilly too, though the wind for some time had got only soft. The curious thing was that I thought of what Grandfather DeWhit had said about beauty. I thought my sister beautiful, and I prepared to ask the old prophet if what I saw was perhaps the answer to his riddle. When I conjured him up, he stood on the hill against the sky and would not answer me.

✻ 18 ✻

MOTHER WAS IN A CHAIR and moaned, "How could she *do* it?" Her face was the way it sometimes was when she would be standing on the back porch helping Nigger Ruth with the wash, drawn up and pleading for consolation with the prophetess. Who many times would embrace her and pat her the way she did Grandmother DeWhit. Of course you knew that it was also the prophetess who said, "Emma and Egan used to come to my house in the old days when I was their original encouragement," and I thought that might have been in Mother's mind when she found Elizabeth's note and cried out first to Nigger Ruth. She said, "Oh my God," as well.

Grandmother DeWhit arrived soon enough to do her brand of consoling which went, "She is only a Fletcher; what else do you expect and-especially-when-the-child-is-so-needful-of-well . . . the child is taking her revenge on us for caring about her, and so let the lost sheep discover its error before it is rescued. We are the ninety-nine," Grandmother sighed fitfully, "and I am tired to death of playing the part of the prodigal's elder brother!"

Mother said, "You have forgotten an awful lot, Mama Mama!"

Grandmother returned, "Oh don't leave me, Emma, don't!"

Mother put on her turban hat. She put on heavy makeup with her hands shaking. Her uncommonly disoriented figure seemed even to cringe from the inside. She was hardly even articulate when she buttoned up her coat and told Grandmother that she was going down to Ruth's to get Elizabeth. The face paint waved, embossed against the firelight of the parlor. Then Mother seemed to have panicked all the way and she had also forced me into my coat. In the dark, the night shadowed by the pines and strung with the customary lights from cars passing on the Vermen road, she pulled me with her down Grandfather's hill while Grandmother called out remaining taunts.

You could hear the brush rip the bottom of Mother's dress. I felt the cockleburs, as well, grab the flesh of my legs, and when we had got to Nigger Ruth's house, Mother knocked without any particular dignity, herself covered with the little brown weeds. She paced until the wave of whispers inside had tempered the door's opening with suspense.

Mother said, "Where is Elizabeth?"

Ruth said, "The child is gone, Emma."

She invited us in and puffed her breath. She held the collar of her dress to her throat, jabbing with an intense index finger.

"But there ain't no cause for alarm," she continued.

Mother kept on her coat, though the prophetess's daughters had each offered to take it. From before the fire they all rushed to comfort her, thin Mascara, simple Acacia, obese Turtledove. Their faces ranged from yellow to dark brown, and they said, "Now Emma."

"*Mrs. Fletcher,*" Mother corrected hesitantly, and while she got her bearings over the movements of her hosts, Ruth herself had invited me aside and smiled and started to pick the cockleburs from my breeches.

"Just tell me where she is, Ruth, and that's all and then I'll take care of it," Mother insisted. And Ruth told her outright that it was no use. She said, "Elizabeth has left three hours ago for the marrying town of Huanebango."

Mother said, "But Ruth, it's Father's child that she's run off with!"

Ruth said, "But honey, you ain't his daughter."

Collapsed into a chair, Mother rubbed her chin.

Ruth looked over to her girls and nodded for them to be seated and become sympathetic. They had it down to become remorseful as well and so in the thick sadness they started to wring their hands properly.

At last Mother said, "Now look, Ruth, you know that Elizabeth is that *way,* and you know that she is only thirteen."

"I married when I was the same."

"Elizabeth's mind hasn't got nothing to do with it."

"Your daughter loves that boy, and she's got the equipment."

Mother said, "Oh, God, no."

Then it was quiet and they all nodded from heads which warmly confirmed each other's diagnosis. They said, "Oh how poor Elizabeth suffered in that house, how she loved her poor Clyde and all."

"And then you and Ella Mae washed her out with cold creme!"

In that dark motion of their evident discernment, Mother appeared to see the light. That or Ruth's powers had caused her to click her fingernails together nervously and for the space of two minutes at least she let herself begin to sob out loud.

"Oh, I just can't leave Mama, and I just can't have the girl running off like that."

She shook also, as she had done earlier, and then, in what seemed a complete surge of repentance, Mother got up and put herself into Ruth's arms next to me.

"Oh Ruth, whatever am I to do?" she sobbed.

"Pray that Egan gets home soon!"

The two women let go their embrace and stared corporately into each other's eyes. Neither smiled though the particular sympathy of it showed as if they were trying to outdo one another in affection. It was, in fact, certain that my mother and Nigger Ruth the Prophetess were kissing and crying out loud.

Mother said, "Oh Aunt Ruth!"

Ruth said, "Sweet child!"

The former's cry went louder then and the instincts which had seemed to fail her earlier prompted her somehow to listen to the air and the little sounds that sucked about the room like a baby nursing. But Mother also seemed trapped. She quizzed Aunt Ruth's wisdom as though it had been major evidence in a crime.

Ruth said, "You don't want to become what your mama is, Emma. The whole town knows how good you have been to her, but you don't want to become *like* her, do you?"

"Oh, no!"

"Then let Elizabeth have her loving."

The yellow woman's eyes rolled and she tried to laugh. "I know all about it," she said, "because years ago before Robert DeWhit ever came to town and before I married Henry Jobson, me and Beans and Ella Mae used to use the bedpost on one another of a Saturday — we wanted a man. That's what *it* does to you. You was born and Ella Mae knew better than Beans and me. But that was loving and she messed it all up when she married old Bob DeWhit. She was the prettiest of us, and the nearest white, and he wanted somebody that could have him a son. You know, Emma, that it was Beans that he loved. It was always Beans, and so leave poor Elizabeth to her loving."

Ruth went to the hearth. She put her hands on the mantel before her. Quite as if her feeling had been built up of words she had only allowed herself to speak out of pity, the prophetess thrust her face quietly into a resolute stare.

"Emma, face your husband," she said, "and face your color!"

Now Grandfather's hill seemed a fitting place to breathe again. The air was secure, but Mother hugged the wind solicitously. She was staring at me cautiously; and she was crying again. I pulled myself up under her arm and next to her so that I could embrace her, and she held on steadily amidst quick attempts to control her dripping face paint, though she had taken some of it and rubbed it in. She lumbered to the fish pond, and she sat down on the ledge, leaving me behind to test my loyalty. She folded her arms on her breast and looked down, playing with her shoes on the ground. Finally she put her hand out to me.

"Your mother doesn't know what to do," she said.

She embraced me.

But once more her face emitted uncommon agencies, lovely ones, it seemed, as the beat of her heart became visible in a rocking thump at the veins of her forehead, under the melting rouge.

I rubbed two fingers to my tongue and tried to remove some of her face paint. I took a swatch of her brush-torn dress then and soaked it in the pond, at length removing the paint as though it were a mask.

She was lovelier.

Her eyes darted like sun spots. She held me as

was her custom, and I did not mind for a while until the power of her movements became uncomfortable. She looked to comfort herself, it seemed, by pushing me inside her body, and then she held me up and twirled from the ledge downward toward the climb of Grandfather's hill. She rolled there with me, laughing, and we stopped in the clearing beneath the special pine tree. I tried to pick up her laughter and raised myself upon her, holding, while she continued alternately to sob and to laugh. It was not pleasant then to have been kissed as she kissed me. Mother said, "Aunt Ruth, Aunt Beans, oh Egan."

From beneath her cold and naked shoulders I ran to my closet. I hid in the dark and I called out to Grandfather DeWhit. "Oh, it was horrible," I said.

* 19 *

THE VERY TENSENESS which she had under the pine tree never left Mother's face when she talked thereafter. The distance of it was almost something that you could feel, and so I answered her with yes or no as simply as I could, though when she looked at me that way, I had a peculiar feeling of not being able either to go forward or reverse.

The next important thing was that she sent me to school. But every day, with that look, she would always ask the same question, "What did you learn in that place to betray me?"

The text book in school was called *Do That Then,* and the teacher was Miss Carlyle, as I had expected. She was a thin jawy woman who wore her hair like a bandage and when she saw all the words I knew, she put me in the first desk beyond everybody else and called

me the Sunflower. Which meant, of course, that nobody talked to me but Miss Carlyle herself, and she
said, "This is the grandson of RSD." When I asked her
the definition of certain words which I supposed being
in school would have allowed me to ask, she put her
hand on my face and suggested that such words as those
were not for poets, and then she whispered, however,
that "really you ought to take it up with someone, say,
like Tolly Butterworth."

Therefore, it was, at long last, Tolly who informed
me:

"Bitch, a woman with hair between her legs."
"Mother and Elizabeth."

"Goddamn, the best word to put in front of bitch."
"Mother and Elizabeth."

"Titty — uh — two of them . . ."
"Mother and . . . uh . . ."

For days she cried when I told her, but I said, "Well
just the same it's what I learned." And she immediately
began to preside over my lessons from *Do That Then*,
though midpoint of each she often started to cry about
Elizabeth or about Father, proposing in a peculiar whisper similar to Miss Carlyle's that the remedy for the
former problem was that word *annulment;* for the
latter, a matter of *intimate behavior.*

Whatever either of the terms meant, Mother finally

did nothing about them but cry and watch the postal deliveries; she was still practicing the piano, and otherwise paced the hallway.

Meantime the season and school only heightened my desire to have Father back. In the first case it was the chill which I felt he would blot out. And in the second, I had many lines for him by then; and I mean they were sometimes lines which Mother refused to help me put into my scrapbook. For instance, that line *he knows the truth* was one which she said ought to be changed to *he sometimes gets things right*. She declined altogether to write *he does well with bottom parts*.

Which means that I had to go back to Tolly Butterworth for what I wanted and he listened to me with encouragement. He put down any word I desired, even those which defined Mother, and then he drew pictures of it so that I could no longer show her the scrapbook.

Tolly helped me write that letter which went

Dear Elizabeth. How are things in the marrying Town of Huanebango?

and so forth.

Then that one which went:

Dear Father. How are you I am fine. And I am going to have you a baseball team. I am in school and I have put down many lines for you although I am just now learning to write enough. I want to go with you and that is all. Your son.

Though Mother continually forbade me to have anything more to do with Tolly, he had always been
around. For instance, he talked to me beside the stop
sign after school, and many times suggested that the
only reason Mother did not want me near him was on
account of her fulfilling the definition of a bitch. When
he wrote those letters for me and was good enough to
find postage stamps and put them into Blaze Burnett's
dray truck, I hardly felt as though he were what
Mother said he was. At last it was specially true that
I got for the moment beholden to Tolly Butterworth
when, very soon, he arrived at the front yard of Grandfather's house and announced that he had got my baseball team. I said, "Wait a minute now," and ran quickly
inside where I put on my father's drawers and my
uniform. I planted my foot on the red wagon and said,
"Bullshit, the motto of this baseball team is bullshit!"

Then the players went away without signing the
contracts which Tolly had prepared. I had mucked it
up, he said, but he was also willing to write a second
letter to Father and say "I, Tolerance Butterworth,
certify that a baseball team was once owned and oper-
ated by Egan Fletcher, Jr., and that, furthermore, the
motto was bullshit."

That was what I wanted, and that was what I got,
and then Tolly walked with me on the driveway, up and
down, to encourage me not to worry. "Oh he'll be home,
and just think of him over there in a green uniform."

My friend held my shoulder with a tight arm and
tugged me back and forth on the driveway.

"So she really did hold you like that under the pine tree?"

"Yes."

Tolly's eyes were a peculiar shade of amber. They moved with less than the authority of Father's but they betrayed a clear anxiety. He looked in many directions at once and rubbed his trouser leg. It was a matter of his rolling his tongue about on his lower lip too, come to think of it, and then it was a matter of his having batted his eyes consistently.

"Your mother, the bitch," he said, "took you under the pine tree for a reason which is good. She was teaching you something."

Tolly fidgeted more or less and then ordered that we must talk about it indoors. He led me to the wood-shed next to the back porch where it was almost dark and where we lay on the floor.

He said, "You see there's that thing called hump which I told you about."

"I remember."

"And the most intense pleasure a man can have is in his pecker. There. Here. If I . . . and then . . . you see?"

Upon his back Tolly moved me to thinking of shadows and charging sensations. He himself fed those shadows. The feeling was in the air, he said, in minute particles.

"Here, see," he said.

"I am ashamed of this and I am afraid," I replied.

"Stupid!"

"But see how I am shaking," I said, "and now I think

I am going to retch. Tolly you should not . . . I am
going to . . . retch!"

"For God'ssakes be still, Egan. Aw, go ahead and
retch. Here."

There was at once the mixture of slimes, I recall,
the spit-up broth of tomato soup and the seeds of corn.
And there was the other sort of slime.

Tolly Butterworth went away from the woodshed
laughing. He went away and complained that I made
him tired, and the unspeakable feeling that governed
my movements when he was gone snapped at my insides
alone. Besides being curious, I was not walking steadily
and then there was all the mess which I did not quite
notice adequately.

Less than cautious, I tried going to my room by the
back of the house, and there you had both Mother and
Grandmother DeWhit staring down at me with more
than their usual measure of knowledge.

"Well," I said, "I have learned how to hump, and
there is the poon."

In the kitchen, Mother cried excitedly that she knew
something like that would happen. She first lamented
the condition of Father's drawers and then she poured
on Clorox by the cupful while Grandmother DeWhit
paraded with the baseball uniform as though it had
been John the Baptist's head and she were Salome.

"I will get the kerosene can first," she proclaimed.
"There is another tree stump out there in back."

And there I was naked and being examined, and

Mother herself took a dishcloth to me. Both the women had been silent and they looked at each other with a special horror.

"But it happens to everybody."

"And shouldn't. The-Lord-only-knows-it-was-Robert-DeWhit's-problem. It-was-Egan-Fletcher's. It-was-silly-Elizabeth's-and-it-was-Wexie-Fletcher's. Now-it's-the-boy's. Thank-God-it's-not-mine!"

Mother shook her head ambivalently and she stood next to me. You could hear her hosiery rubbing together under the housedress while she apparently tried to think of the right thing. In a curious way, her face spoke a certain new dependence, as if she were in an entreaty, and she frowned. She tried these words: "Well, now you know," in an almost soft and pleading manner, while her eyes darted in many directions. The sense of dependence grew, thereupon, in her gestures of restraint which included a sudden very deep sigh. Then she had put out her arms to me more pleadingly than ever but I did not go there. Her face must have wilted even to the point of looking displaced.

Mother quickly enough fetched me some clean clothes, then, and sat with Father's wet drawers in her lap, staring at me, as I dressed. The sun in the room was particularly appropriate for her thick and heavy breathing, itself being both bright and overpowering. Nonetheless, she finally ordered that I was not to be in that condition again, and with Grandmother she said a momentary prayer, their first together in a long while, and straightened her dress. All these moments Mother did not once seem sure of what she was about, I repeat, and in fact she ultimately had to rely on Grandmother DeWhit to convince her that she was doing the right thing.

✳ 20 ✳

THAT IS ULTIMATELY HOW we wound up at Sheba's Beauty Parlor that day, which by Grandmother's prescription was the adequate place to reward herself and Mother for having endured *my* ordeal in the woodshed. As it was Saturday, they had already planned a trip there anyhow, but, presently, on account of what they designated *obvious reasons*, they elected to have me go along too.

The clear chill in my feelings was adequately matched by a building which was cold and the downstairs of the Purina Dog Chow Store. You had the round-cornered oak veneer partitions separating the parts of this beauty parlor, and shelves which displayed lotions and fingernail files. There was an oval mirror without a frame. And there were permanent wave machines, two of which Annie Lou Hartell, the beautician, clamped promptly to Mother's and Grandmother's heads. The long black wires of the machines came off a treelike pole with their prongs attached to individually wrapped wisps of hair, and then they had their faces covered with something which was like Dutch Cleanser.

Watching me carefully, even through her mask, Grandmother DeWhit commenced the usual type of chatter. "Well, Annie Lou, there-is-not-anything-new-under-the-sun," she said, running the words together in her new form.

"Madam, you are right I'm sure."

"But I mean just as soon as my Robert died like that the whole world collapsed as it did for Cleopatra after Antony. You understand that I wish I had an asp."

"Oh now, Missus DeWhit, you know you don't mean that!"

"Oh indeed I do, for now my life is done without Robert, and Emma threatens an act of which there is only a perfidian ending."

Grandmother's face under the cleanser even showed her mockery. Her eyes, at least, went over to Mother in the other chair. And Mother, in turn, grunted her displeasure. She was stiff about it and seemed elsewhere.

"Oh, Mama," she said.

"But truly," Grandmother continued, "truly it is true that my household is dishonest." She whispered, "You heard about that child Elizabeth, Annie Lou, and her problem with . . . l-o-v-e; you heard about all the rest, and now it seems that the manchild, the one over *there* in the chair, Robert's heir, has started to behave strangely too. The child" — her hands went out in a rounding motion and she lowered them about her groin in a little jerk — "you see? *It* is the problem for so-many-people-I-wonder-dear-Annie-Lou-why-*I*-have-never-been-so-afflicted."

"Uh — madam, I'm sure I don't know."

"And take Emma Ruth there, as well, or my sister Beans (of course *she* stole Robert from *me* and had that silly child which is a disgrace and a b-a-s-t-a-r-d) or even Ruth the Prophetess. They can't control. They have *no* control, Annie Lou, dear. Thank God I had my fling. Thank God it was over for me when I was uh — younger."

Mother let her go on with it indulgently and Miss Hartell, likewise indulgent, had carefully modified the wirings of the permanent wave machine so that she had the proper slack.

Miss Hartell had chickenlike buttocks, which she twisted with little effort and wore like a bustle. And she went back and forth as if she were a nurse taking temperatures, from one of her patients to the other, fetching magazines for Grandmother, and curiously interested, it seemed, in having the DeWhit women as far apart as possible. She turned one chair in one direction and the other in another, only then to have Grandmother insist that she wanted to be able to *see* Mother, especially to *see* me.

I sat in one of the black, chrome-armed waiting chairs, on the edge, and rubbed my hands on my legs. There was nothing to do for the time being but look around, and I got the curious feeling that the walls of the beauty parlor were somehow false, or that they were hollow and contained inner panels which were filled with peculiar laughter and sighs. I heard, for instance, the buzz of an unknown machine which was coming from the ceiling, and then I heard in the back a sound which was like sloshing water in a washtub. Miss Hartell kept going back there through the curtains which separated the rear of the place from the front and each time she returned to check Mother's and Grandmother's condition, she would sidle herself past me smiling and winking with wet hands.

Finally Miss Hartell emerged from the back with a little pink soap dish for me. On the soap dish was a horseshoe magnet which she claimed would pick up hairpins at two feet. She said, "I'll give you ten cents, then, if you'll get down into the floor and get all the hairpins up. Put the black ones in one side of the dish and the brown ones in the other."

I told her "Very well," and I then got down on my knees, under Grandmother's watchful eye, and started dividing the pins, like soldiers, according to rank and color. There were many of them, it turned out, and I made a game of finding the ones which were hidden under corners or stuck beneath the molding. Eventually I took some of the brown pins and twisted them together so that they would stand up. I put a black one against them in battle, and it was Father. He went at the brown pins and chased them off, and then I had him carrying his lance and his spear. On my back for the moment, I was able to go with him into the forest where the soldiers were.

I had in mind the woodshed, and the air was heavy in the beauty parlor. Daddy Egan's face, as usual, was only clear when he moved in and out like the light. The image there did not speak, but finally he was saying, "I will be home." I was on his stomach then and I touched the soft hairs on my arm in order to remember the sensation of it, the special soft movement. How little Mother and Grandmother knew about how the air moved or how feelings came and went, I thought. How silly they were in the beauty chairs with their faces that way.

But Grandmother DeWhit soon enough had reared forward as much as the permanent wave machine would allow and she said, "Child, what are you doing over there on your stomach behind a chair? Come out of there and show me the front of your breeches."

For all the strangeness of hearing those sighs in the walls and the terrible little buzz of whatever the machine was, I had heard Grandmother's words as though they were a screech. There came a burst of energy into my insides which on account of those thoughts of Father had also become distressed. I listened to the movements which then suggested that all of what I was looking at was somehow not true. I was not in a game like a child, it seemed, though Grandmother's insistent voice had approximated a Bingo caller's drone. When I did not answer her immediately she looked as if she might get out of the chair and carry the permanent wave machine with her.

I said, "Grandmother, you are so silly," and then I crawled, as she had asked, from behind the chair. I spread the front of my trousers for her to look at.

"Just don't worry about it," I continued, almost contemptuously, and she sent Annie Lou Hartell to check. Who, embarrassed, I suppose, waddled to see and said, "Uh, well, uh." When Grandmother had sat back again, the beautician sidled closer and whispered, offhand, "Your grandmother is a funny one, but I know your problem." She shook her breasty top and giggled. At last she pinched me and I poured all the pins back onto the floor deliberately.

I was absolutely defiant in it and they were all somehow unsure in their voices. Chattering and somehow moaning at the same time while you heard the collection of *s*'s. Calling me impudent by and large, threatening to punish and then, at last, codifying the speech with reason:

Just-like-a-man-who-must-have-his-pleasure, like-Robert-if-the-truth-were-known (even-though-he-was-less-like-other-men-than-that-animal-Egan-Fletcher). It-is-the-corruption-of-the-family-and-now-the-boy-too, now-the-heir-of-this-estate-of-which-there-can-be-only-one-heir and I swear I just don't know and-

"Oh, please hush up," I cried. My confidence had got shored up again by the former image of Father in his uniform and then old Grandfather came in too and stood there specially amused that Grandmother DeWhit was in the face cream. And the two of us, less interested in the women's reaction than put upon by their anger, laughed in a new kind of triumph. Grandmother DeWhit, seeing me stare into the ceiling once more, had got infuriated because she thought I was ignoring her, though Mother, whose interest all along continued to be a more indulgent one, had got the final attention. She shushed us all and then pointed with alarm to the front door of the beauty parlor which opened and produced a resentful and frightened Blaze Burnett, the drayman. He was holding a crumpled yellow paper in his hand and then he gasped as well and rolled his eyes.

Amidst the sounds of straightening girdles and hosiery and even the faint patting of excited throats, he looked around the room and said, "Now Missus Fletcher, don't get excited nor nothing like that."

"For God'ssakes, what is it?" Mother said.

"Egan's got himself killed in Poland," Mr. Burnett said.

There you had it that Mother's cries went up like quacks of geese and she scraped off the face cream and pulled her hair madly from the permanent wave machine. Her voice collected, it seemed, the fury of all her former cries, while Grandmother DeWhit, as though her remark had been selected for the occasion, said, "Well-now-he's-dead-in-Poland, and at last!"

The otherwise cold beauty parlor was like a collapsing

tin box and the sides rattled so that the Purina man yelled down that the noise was upsetting his collie pups. But the situation, perhaps constricted as the women's confusion itself, was one which I only looked at out of desperation. I did not try to name my idea of Father with his lance and his spear. In the same manner by which I had not believed Grandfather gone when he did what they said and *died*, I did not either believe it of the brown gentleman who had left me just moments before. Old Grandfather assured me eminently too, shaking his head like a monkey's, that it was only just Mother's peculiar notion of beauty which now caused her to misunderstand. As for Grandmother De-Whit, he said that she had got to be left to heaven anyhow. And he said, "She's strictly a case for God, for the Infinite Ply."

Coming off that recollection, I must have tried to persuade Mother of my idea, but when she would not listen at all, I went and buried my face in her lap where instinct, I suppose, told me I would do the most good.

✳ 21 ✳

AND SO YOU SEE he was supposed to be dead too and he was supposed to have come by it with a mortar wound, or so the telegram went on. Father was *not* dead, but of course, and as usual, they did not listen to me when I told them that there was really only one Daddy Egan and he had said that he would come back. My feelings aside, the house buzzed with people coming with gifts, and even of newspaper personnel who had taken photographs of Mother and reported it:

TRAGEDY IN THE SOUTH
THE HORROR OF IT
BUT ONE MORE FATALITY
HITLER'S FOLLY

Nigger Ruth had come to do the cleaning and she comforted in most cases better than Mrs. Violet Brendelle who was trained to do that sort of thing. Whereas Mrs. Brendelle came there looking sad and quickly putting her arms around Mother (who might finally have cried herself out) and eventually crying as well and getting Mother once more frantic, Ruth said, "Well they's worse things than dying and at least you and Egan have loved."

We had brought Mother home from the beauty parlor exhausted and with less hair. Her face had got coarser too, from the blend of face cream which had not quite come off all the way. Ruth removed that strikingly so that Mother lay in the bed eventually looking lovely and very quiet. Mr. Burnett, the drayman, in an almost contemptuous manner, had got the doctor and the Reverend and they delivered both Mother and Grandmother DeWhit to new stares and went away. Then Mother would not see anyone else but Grandmother and Nigger Ruth and me. She especially refused any contact with the Fletchers of Vermen though Grandmother Willie Fletcher and my three aunts came over daily in the farm pickup and sat in the foyer apart from everyone else. Grandmother Fletcher had almost angrily said that he ought to be buried in his own town and when Mother was told of it, she raced to the stairs and ordered that ushers be carefully selected for round-the-clock duty. Otherwise she did nothing but lie in bed and plot with her stare until, weeks later, they brought in the coffin. Then she began to cry. Then she made her plans and had a new stiffness in avoiding the Fletchers. She held my hand continually and said, "If only it had not been in the wintertime! If only not in the cold beauty parlor!"

Mother went and composed a clarinet quintet, which was the first of her plans to bury him properly, and she engaged five high school musicians in red and black uniforms to sit there like radiator pipes and play it. It so sounded like the "Black Hawk Waltz," and then you had, in the jaundiced parlor, this feeble blend of the flowers and the box and the tune.

Mother also put up a sign which read *Mrs. Fletcher, wife of Egan Fletcher, requests that no one touch the remains.*

She herself would not go near him.

Much of the time before the arrival of the box, I had talked to old Grandfather about it, telling him that I did not understand; and as his response was "Here I am the living proof," I told Mother his words. She first looked entirely frightened, and then oh so put off. She said, "This is the same business that you have thought about your grandfather and it must stop. I encourage you to write lines, but you cannot have ghosts in the house."

It was futile to argue with her or any of the rest of the Christian people who came and went over to her and said, "We are sorry." Sometimes I went in there and walked up to one or two of the strangers and said, "But you don't know the truth. I have my father's letter and he says absolutely that he will be back.

Now I can only imagine his face, but soon I will see it clearly."

"Ha, ha," they said, all of them, including the Reverend Brendelle who came reluctantly every morning on account of not being certain of the DeWhits' continued devotion. So, while the box was still there, the last evening before they were supposed to start Mother's special design of a funeral, I went pointblank into the parlor and climbed into it and said, "Well, you let me know when you are ready to say what you have to."

Father looked no different than I had remembered him and I undid the top of his uniform two notches and put my head on his shoulder. It was hard and cold, but my breath on it had made it grow warm. On his unmoving arm, as well, I looked to discover a forest through which to play at seeing what was before me. The shades of the candles were not altogether the fitting ones, though they burned with a less perfect coloring effect than the sun on the balustrade. I imagined him on the former days and especially that night before he had gone away. I remembered his speech and the words, which had eluded me, concerning what was called *doing love*. I wanted to tell him what Tolly had done and I wanted to speak somehow of what I had felt, but Mr. Burnett had come in then horrified and he brought two other ushers who helped him take me away to bed. He lamented my grief, he said, and though I tried to explain that I had not been crying, he only carefully said that it was just like Egan and Egan ought to have a son just like that. "My heavens," said Mr. Burnett, "you know your father had been riding back and forth with me for almost fifteen years. He was rich, and he might have an automobile, but he always hitched. Don't you think that that is something (and your mother has treated him rotten)?"

"Well, sir," I said, confused, and I slept until they had come for me to hold Mother's hand and go with her to face the ceremony where of course the great flute players had showed up as before.

Aunt Ruth was there with the rest of us, and Mother specially embraced her and then Great-aunt Beans. But she did not embrace any of the Fletchers from the town of Vermen. She only shook Aunt Wexie's hand and then looked unpleasantly at Grandmother Fletcher and the others.

Grandmother DeWhit breathed with her heavily and sniffed.

Aunt Ruth picked me up and stood beside Mother and then she cried and held me up next to her face and rocked me back and forth.

Elizabeth and Clyde made their entry from the marrying town of Huanebango as well, one which startled everybody. And Elizabeth looked so much like Mother that you had to look twice, her face well-powdered and older, and she had her hair in an up-sweep. Beneath the tears she seemed to show her self-vindication.

As for Clyde, he was in a corduroy suit. It fitted

nicely and he was trim. He had a haircut and there was no pelvic bulge to speak of.

When Mother looked at Elizabeth and him, she did it with quick glances or not at all. She did not stop crying.

It was what the Reverend said that sustained the funeral into a lengthy affair, for Mother's prescriptions had only to do with decoration. The sermon ran into a near hour's worth of newspaper quotes, though the Reverend had been careful to edit. I can remember that there was hardly a move at all in the Memorial Church and hardly a noise but those which came from the still broken organ blower. The box itself, its black felt cover splotched with many fingerprints, was perhaps even a little askew on its moorings, and the point is that they were ready at last to bury him with his face lightly turned and his hair in the condition I had left it. You saw the sober little lines at his mouth almost move with the discomfort of at last being locked up there and carried in the same fashion which they had used for Grandfather. It was all very slow, all very careful, and Mother had planned it well.

She had it so that they went their way to the cemetery in a special cortege according to what she had determined as only proper, the cortege an elegant train in which the box was on the shoulders of ushers such as Uncle Fred Duncan and a man who Nigger Ruth said was the radio sportsman. There were buglers and the flag was draped over the box, then, while those men in their uniforms raised their swords and so forth. Soon came as well the clarinet players on a flat-bed truck followed by the Reverend and his group, all in step, adequately inclined to tears and other noises.

Then in the rear followed Grandmother Fletcher and Aunt Wexie and the others, obviously still annoyed. They appeared to have no use even for the buglers and so Mother continued to ignore them. Dressed in black, she came wobbling forward, steadied by Mr. Burnett who fed her handkerchiefs.

They put the box down with its flowers and everything seemed drained out like a headward gully. Faces were in general confused, but everybody was soon enough aware that the Fletchers were angry. Aunt Wexie's tears were not merely sorrowful and Grandmother Fletcher stood there and slapped her foot on the ground.

At length the woman seemed slowly to grow enraged. She listened to the music which went on in a steady drum, the same repetition by those students who themselves seemed to hold the music in contempt. The air was greased with a sort of distrust, and Mother went up to tie the gold cord, which she had invented, around the box before its descent.

That, I remember, had been the last straw for Grandmother Fletcher.

She went up there beside Mother and tore off the cord and threw it on the ground.

"This here stuff is nonsense and I won't have it for

Joonie!" She faced Mother exactly and pulled up her veil.

She said, "Stop them children playing the sousaphones, Emma, as I've got something to say!"

Mother cringed, though the furor itself had already caused the musicians to stop playing. The old woman, wearing her long dress and her customary necklace, attacked the flowers next, which were promptly scattered like marbles. Then she had been very plain and stood there in the middle of the plot crying. Her face had only the plaintive look of someone terribly hurt and all the great flute players stood tall and began to ponder.

"Now, uh, uh, Mrs. Fletcher," the Reverend said.

And she said, "Austin Brendelle, you know this ain't right."

She faced the crowd and her hands were up in entreaty.

"Joonie Fletcher was a simple man. He didn't believe in such as this stuff, nor the DeWhits. You see don't you that Emma there has taken everything from him and give him nothing. Joonie was never untrue to her neither. Now she wants to bury him like *that*. I'm taking my Joonie home."

Without further hesitation Grandmother Fletcher turned again in Mother's direction where she was met with outrage. She called Wexie and Maggie and Myra to her side and told the crowd that *she* was taking the box and that *she* was going to bury him in Vermen.

The four of them proceeded to lift the coffin with a

struggle, though for the moment they bore the weight elegantly. There was intense silence and not even the Reverend Brendelle came up and said stop. When they had got the box nearly in front of Mother, where they stopped briefly and wept, Great-uncle Fred Duncan went to them and took an entire end. For the nonce, he virtually glowered at Grandmother DeWhit as well.

"Come *with* us," Grandmother Fletcher whispered to Mother. She stood there plaintively and guileless, her mouth constricted to hold back the tears.

Mother only wept on. She looked at Grandmother DeWhit, who, without any warning, fell to the ground in a faint.

Then Mother was crying, "Oh, Mama, oh, Mama," and she turned back to the Fletchers and screamed, "Look what you've done . . . I was giving Egan a fitting burial, an elegant one; one better than yours, one better . . . whores!" She cried it, "Whores, whores," out loud.

At that moment the Reverend first turned his back on her, and he took his part of the coffin too; then Mrs. Brendelle, then more people than could get hold of it took a part of the coffin. Those who did not help out stood and gaped, and it was borne aloft quickly to the farm truck in which the Fletcher women had arrived.

I ran after them, called to by Mother. I stood midway between Aunt Wexie and her while the former tried to smile and lift the coffin. I turned back to Mother and I saw that she was crying alone and Grandmother

DeWhit was lying there alone. Mother's look was heightened beyond any former expression altogether. She called out, "Oh Egan, darling, my blessed Egan, my . . ."

She stooped in a degrading position then, pulling her dress up nearly to her hips so that she could lift Grandmother DeWhit. Her stare remained, though she whispered to herself. Ultimately she stumbled and fell and no one came.

I went to my mother and she sat down on the ground. I tried to get her to rise and I called out to Grandmother DeWhit to wake up. Neither of them moved at all until Nigger Ruth arrived, at last Aunt Beans too, who each affirmed that Grandmother would be over it soon.

They said, "What has happened is only right."

In the distance, even Elizabeth had followed the Fletcher truck, her arms around Aunt Wexie, nearly dancing exuberantly. She and Clyde looked back toward us, though their special stare had been given to Grandmother as she slowly began to wake up.

It seems pointless to call attention to the automatic loyalties which were formed in the exchange, but it is nonetheless true that my mother, having had the next moment lucid, had got up and raved against the people whom she regarded as tormentors. It was to everyone that she cried her condemnations and said, "whores," while Grandmother DeWhit smiled warmly.

"Take him off that way if you feel like that," Mother cried. "You can have your silly house and Egan's silly game of baseball."

"By all means," Grandmother said, and to the side she buzzed in a soft whisper to Aunt Ruth, "and-of-course-you-know-Ruth-the-real-reason-behind-this-whole-thing-which-is-that-poor-Emma-was-led-astray-under-the-pine-tree-and-if-she-had-waited-long-enough-there-would-have-been-someone-besides-a-Fletcher-heir-and-some-one-who-would . . ."

It was exactly four-thirty in the afternoon, I remember, when winter was coming on full that the air maneuvered those hundreds of people away. It was frigid cold, in fact, and we closed up the windows of the Jonesgay Family Car as it once more ascended the driveway to Grandfather's house. Mother clutched me helplessly in the back seat and she said, "You are really all I have."

Grandmother DeWhit touched me sweetly as well.

The moment gave away to a festive suppertime, though no one ate. The three of us, and Nigger Ruth, looked at each other in aversion, but we tried to smile. I thought just of Father and wondered if he might have been displeased with me.

When Mother started to cry and wail as she had in the beauty parlor, when she commenced to dance with Grandmother and moan, "Oh what are *we* going to do?" I said, "Hush up, the both of you," just as before, and this time they did.

✳ 22 ✳

THERE WERE PASSING LIGHTS and dependencies, and the days ahead must have had to be measured by them. Mother did not at all wash her face, nor did Grandmother, and the news was that Grandmother Fletcher had put the box amongst lilacs in her backyard. This is true, but what mattered was not that. Mother and Grandmother did not care, and I awaited my own outcomes as well, while Mother kept reminding me, "You are your grandfather's heir, and *that* is the thing."

I did not argue with her as she sat at the piano every morning and practiced the "Black Hawk Waltz." Her eyes were fixed and glassy at that point, and she did not really care to say anything more.

Aunt Ruth came and looked at her condition and then she moved into Grandfather's house which pleased Grandmother on account of the linens and the wash, and then pleased Mother on account of the back rubs.

For days thereafter, I went to the linen closet and waited for Father to come to me again. This was the important thing; and I wanted him to come desperately. I talked about it to Daddy Robert, and he told me to be patient, and he told me politely that he was upset that I had not figured out his riddle yet. I said, "For God's-sakes, what in the world can *I* do?"

Ruth came and said, "Now, child, it is not going to be easy, but it will be O.K."

"What does it all mean, Nigger Ruth?"

"Well, it means that for a while you are going to have to worry a little bit."

"But about what, Nigger Ruth?"

"Well, your mother is not quite going to be the same."

"I see."

"Well, your grandmother depends so on your mama."

"Very well."

"Well, you, child, is the one which will have to wait until you have grown up. You is the heir."

I put myself into her arms and she carefully touched my face. She did not touch me elsewhere and I was surprised. I held Aunt Ruth's hand and told her about Father and about the woodshed. She laughed and then said that Tolly Butterworth already had run off to Charlottesville.

"That boy weren't interested in you," she said, "but he told you right."

I said, "Will I not ever see Tolly?"

"Prob'ly not, child."

"What about Elizabeth?"

"Maybe sometime, but only after a while. Meantime, it's good that you remember your daddy. If you say he's coming back, then he is. You remember your daddy and then you keep going to school and things will be O.K."

Ruth's yellow face then had contained all its former charm and I took her at her word and went back to the closet. I took out my scrapbook and tried to think of the words for it, and then I tried to imagine Father once again in battle with his lance and his spear. I did not like only imagining him. And I rested impatiently, wishing that I had my baseball uniform, wishing that Mother had not taken the drawers away. I could then but recall the face in the box and the crisp chill of its flesh as I heard Mother outside in the parlor practicing her piano piece.

Then Great-aunt Beans and Great-uncle Fred were at the door first with the information that everything was well at the DeWhit Industries in Cotton in Kornelius-Above-the-South-Shoals; that Uncle Fred had closed the deals on new money; that perhaps there was even a chance of such and such. And Mother was determinedly unreceptive as she stared glassily from her place on the piano bench. Grandmother DeWhit as well stood beside the fireplace with her arm on the mantel and groaned that she was putting up with them just barely.

"Why did you go and help them with that coffin?" Mother said.

And Fred said, "It was only right, Emma, as Egan belonged to them. He wasn't a DeWhit; he wasn't one of you."

"You humiliated me," she cried.

"You needed it," he only said coldly.

And then Mother stared the more, playing with a string and making a cat's cradle in the corner. Uncle Fred laced up the tops of his shoes as he waited then in silence, and he examined Aunt Beans beside him as if he had never done so before. At length the two of them had a look which suggested that they really had come for other purposes, and finally it was Great-aunt Beans herself who said, "Now about Elizabeth and Clyde, should we let them be or should we get one of them *ammulnents.*"

Grandmother DeWhit could not resist, "*Annulment*, you silly woman."

Stares enveloped the uncertain faces and they were looking at Mother. Fred told her sympathetically that he and Beans had been thinking about it a long time, and then Beans said, "But we know that the marriage has already been consumed."

"Consummated," said Grandmother DeWhit.

And then Fred said, "Well, whatever, the girl's fucked by now."

And that word fucked in general had caused attention to focus on Mother again, who quickly was grimacing over it. She was as well, by then, occupied by a rhythm that she made with her foot. Twined about her hands she held her cat's cradle still and she snapped it as though it were rubber. At first she only said, "If this does not bother me, I don't see why it should bother you. I mean, the two of them are worthless because of what they did, I mean they had to — forget the annulment," Mother said.

You could see her assuming a plane of indifference. She drew, as if removing a glove, a sudden inside blackness about herself and she quite resolutely started to gape around the room. Which visibly frightened both Great-aunt Beans and her husband. Nigger Ruth came in and held her, and she stood engagingly and looked at her guests as though they had been rival beauty queens.

Fred said, "Emma, we just must face it that the girl has been fucked and you are wise to say what you have. You are wise and . . ."

"Get out of here," Mother said. She said, "So the child has been . . . *violated*. So?"

"Fucked, Emma, fucked!"

Once again the sound of the word had seemed to thicken the air. Then Aunt Beans giggled while she looked at Mother, stuffing her great buttocks, as much as possible, the more carefully into a crevice between the sofa's edge and the pillow where she sat. She braced up her bosom like a tapestried virgin.

I said, "What does this word *fuck* mean?"

They answered antiphonally, "Hush up, child." And the laughter between Fred and Beans had been consummate, though Grandmother DeWhit had fled in terror. Mother, herself, with her head down, had put the nail of her index finger between her front teeth, only eventually to look up with a slight smile. She let go Aunt Ruth's hand and stretched her arms up wildly, and then she danced a little and sang, "Loo, loo, loo, da, dadada-dada,da,da,da,da,dah,da,dah. Tell me Beans, dear," she said, "did you truly used to use the bedpost on Mama, you and Ruth? How many ways did you and *Father* know?"

Great-aunt Beans's face got blanched and Aunt Ruth tried to shush Mother deliberately.

"No," Mother snapped, and her former smile blossomed to laughter. Almost triumphantly, she said, "*Fuck* is not really a bad term for it at all. It rhymes with *luck* which in turn is the word both for fortune and chance. It was chance that ruined us, wasn't it? The DeWhits have been ruined by chance. Noblesse oblige is gone. *Duty* has kept me from being happy; my beauty is gone as well; at last, then, my love is dead. Egan is dead!"

Then Mother twirled endlessly, and the rhyme which she sang was this:

> Fortune you importune
> But you fuck with luck!

She danced gaily and even made a tune for it. She said, "Smart child, put it in your scrapbook and there will be others, others to come: years of them!"

Mother ascended the stairs saying other rhymes such

as those there, and such as those which she still says today. And perhaps I need not say that at that moment I had wished Daddy Egan back uncontrollably. While the others dispersed in the ambivalence which has since pervaded the DeWhit household, and at Ruth's request and according to her methods, I went to my linen closet and cried out for him. Ruth followed and put me into her arms where she only just rubbed my face again. The vapor of her breath was sweet while she held me that time, and I wondered that she had not first spoken some prophecy before she said that she had better go and get back to the wash.

✳ 23 ✳

It was settled that Mother played best not only the "Black Hawk Waltz," but as well the many pieces in the nine red volumes of the Scribner's Listen and Hear It Library, though she often complained that there was a mistake in the b-flat of the fifth stave of John Field's "Nocturne" in that key. And Grandmother, having been sustained eminently by Mother's recitals, carefully attended to the Sacred Bolts while she listened and criticized. She went back to praying and winding her clocks just as she does today.

Grandfather's house was silent but for the sound of the piano and those clocks, and nobody came. I left every morning from Aunt Ruth's arms and went out to school where slowly, in those days, the words which were offered in *Do That Then* (along with those I already knew) became the ones which I used to begin my favorite lines:

Father does seem
to be here
and he moves in the air
somewhere
he is
the hair
which lies
underneath the earth
and grows out.

He did not come, though I waited patiently and
though old Grandfather for the nonce said, "Be even
more patient and just make sure that you are in the
right place." And with Ruth's permission I went often
to the closet. I often simply imagined him, thus, still
waiting somewhere in the forest or upon the sun, as if
he might finally have at least descended that far.

Mother came in saying, "Fuck, fuck, fuck, fuck," and
there she was looking at me with a grand omniscience,
giving me permission to say that word *titty* if I wished
— as often or in whatever circumstances I might
choose — and I said, "Titty, titty, titty, titty."

"See there," she said, "that no thunderbolt struck you
and that you did not displease me."

She blinked upward too, her face the mere shadow of
former beauties, and I was aware that she had got very
tired and old. Days afterward, she would bring her
rhymes to me in the closet (when she had done with
her practice) and I would listen, though finally I had
only become used to them. And if not that, she oftener

went to Nigger Ruth who comforted her by saying
Noblesse oblige. But the point is that Mother had even-
tually decided that I was not going to leave her ever.
She said, in so many words, "You are mine again."

In her better moments she held me and told me that,
and I did not know what to say. When she was that
near, you knew that she only intended to have it said
so that finally she could go and sit awhile or else play
the piano. Eventually she and Grandmother DeWhit
would be aloft the piano bench together discussing
the weather. At length Grandmother said, "I suppose
I ought to go now and pray for public morality."

That was the sameness of it, and I got all the more
used to going to the closet where I would make up other
lines, and where, with Grandfather, I talked of my
father again.

> "Maybe he will come back in the parlor just as you
> came in the hallway?"
> "Likely not."
> "Maybe in the woodshed?"
> "Certainly not."
> "On Mother's bed?"
> "Not in a million years."
> "Oh, Grandfather, I wish him back, and I wish him
> back this moment!"

Outside you heard the soft flutter of Mother's feet
and the slam of the front door. You heard the sound
of the dray truck off in its rattle. There was at once a
thump at the piano and two major chords. And when I

went out there I found Mother crying on her piano bench and rubbing her eyes and then turning her feet on their toes under her housedress.

Mother was holding a letter. It was dirty and worn and old, its air mail colors even faded. And this letter, she cried, lucidly and without rhyme, was from Daddy Egan. Mother held it forward without giving it to me, as though, first, she intended to be quite secret. She giggled somehow in the midst of strange little whimpers and the clockwise movement of her head. She threw her uncombed hair into a rope while staring.

"What does it say?" I asked.

But Mother pretended bewilderment, lightly straightening the fit of her housedress and putting out her fingers to look at them.

"This," she said, bearing up the letter, "this, goddamnit, is his last word to us before, and . . . oh-if-it-isn't-late-like-everything-else!"

Mother seemed to go on with her weeping again, but you could not tell and then she pressed the envelope into her face and blew on it. She finally batted it in the air with her fingers and went away.

The sober act faded like the swish of her housedress though it left the foyer where I stood cold as the marble floor itself. I had my scrapbook in my hands and a little note from Miss Carlyle directing Ruth to help me learn the word *laugh*. I worked intently to understand. I had in mind to take the letter and try to read it. Hearing only the sound of my shoes against the floor, and feeling the sudden chill which somehow pretended to dominate the room as well, I did reach down and take the envelope. I put my scrapbook aside and went to the closet again where, in the customary way, I leaned against the Kirby vacuum in the corner.

It is very simple that what I could read of Father's letter said:

> How are you I am fine, here in
>   my duty.   I would like to
> be home   and I may not be
> home.
> boy thanks for the   team
> But I do not know if I will be home.

I lay there and sobbed and in my head the wild and obscure fears which I was used to came in gushes. The feeling was of the sun dimmed, of a wilted brown mass of color, and of the face no longer willing to come when I wished it to. Even the letter itself could not have been moving.

I threw it into the air as well and then outside Mother and Grandmother DeWhit were sitting together on the piano bench again, ever so attentive to the womanly aspects of their behavior.

"How long has it been?"

"Forever."

"I understand well the pain of your loss."

"And I yours, but we must not let it destroy the finer things. Father had his faults, hadn't he?"

"And Egan his. As I understand it, it were better

that now he has died, for he had many such faults. The grave marker might well read WHO HAD HIS FAULTS."

The coldness of their words was even more frightening and with all my energy I went out to them and told them that they were wrong. They smiled at me graciously and answered that they knew they were. In Mother's eyes at last appeared the look of obedience which she has always had since then, and she said, "Whatever you say, dear." She was not crying. She held Grandmother's hand and kissed her and made a rhyme. They played a duet whose rhythm beat on the air like hens' wings against a weasel, and you felt the permanence of it as though it were yet the second thing in the world that would never change.

I folded Daddy Egan's letter into my trousers pocket. Once more in the closet I called loudly for Grandfather, and he did not appear. I tried not to be frightened into thinking that he had gone as well. And it seemed that all the events that I could remember were coming before me and passing into my feelings again. There was the singular day of Father's arrival, and there were those words like *doing love*, and that word *titty*. At last I thought of Grandfather DeWhit well enough too, especially of being that time on his stomach. The old prophet's riddle came at last to mind also. And for that, I was even inclined to take out my scrapbook where I fashioned into a fresh page three pillars of a design which seemed suitable: duty, beauty, truth. In the same convergence I imagined Father as he had been on the night he had done love with Mother. I imagined the woodshed.

My own skill was forthright, though it was subtle; and it was a world suddenly comprehensible in its simplicity, beyond words and figures which on the page imposed themselves as a steamy presence upon my whole body. In the pleasure of it, I think that I repeated the words as if I had understood them as well as I do today, and the rhythm swayed ordinately, as it should have, like all the forges of my life:

> duty, beauty, truth
> duty, beauty, truth
> one without U,T,Y
> another less B,U,T,Y
> the last missing TRU
>
> in line they are th'Infinite Ply
>
> Ply, ply, ply, ply . . .

"Oh God, oh Grandfather, oh Father." I said it in the issuance of my feeling, yet in the finest remembrance of my father's attention. My arms were cold, but I sensed especially the little grains of hair present on them. They sustained me as before, though for whole moments I had wanted to attach them once again to Father.

Then I was exhausted. Then I was thinking that I had come finally to know everything else in the world; I said to myself that I knew what it was to be a hair. I lay against the wall and breathed in that fashion which has sustained me in my grandfather's house ever since.

On the wall in the air without the light came my dreamlike host and I saw that it was Father. I was aware that it was all in those earliest days of my being alive, those first of my waking sensibilities, that he smiled and stood before me. It was as in former times, as he had been on the church balustrade or especially at the train station in Vermen where I first saw him. He was large, and the brown hair fell in a muted yellow light about his face. His face, as formerly pockmarked, had got smooth and iridescent. He smiled.

"There you are," he said.

"Here I wouldn't be if you hadn't left me with *them!*"

"Well, now you know what it was like for me."

"Yes, sir."

Father laughed aloud and put out his hand. He pulled me forward and I felt the tight grasp of his arm. He reached around me quietly and said, "Son."

I said, "I've not done anything right."

He said, "That's not true, for you could hardly leave her."

Father laughed consummately, or I must say now, he laughed in that way that he did on the sofa when he said, "If you saw, you saw."

And I said, "Anyway, it doesn't matter now. I have my lines and I have you and Grandfather."

I knelt before Father, and he kissed my hands. Which he drew up to his face so amicably as to sustain warmth and a kind of liquid nearness.

"Egan, son," he said.

And I carefully removed his shirt. I removed his trousers too, his great white starched drawers, his shoes. I held him tightly, my face ensconced in his belly, and my nose rubbed like so many waves upon the netted hair of his stomach.

"Father," I whispered. "Father. We must go now and you must teach me how to pitch and catch a few."

He held his hands in my hair, and at length fingered my shoulders, unerringly pressing them where his hands seemed the blocks of missing bones.

"Whatever you wish, son," he said.

And I said, "Father."